60
FARRAR
STRAUS
GIROUX

D1125616

SELECTED WORKS OF YASUNARI KAWABATA

The Scarlet Gang of Asakusa

The Dancing Girl of Izu and Other Stories

Snow Country

The Master of Go

A Thousand Cranes

The Sound of the Mountain

The Lake

First Snow on Fuji

The House of the Sleeping Beauties

The Old Capital

Beauty and Sadness

Palm-of-the-Hand Stories

Palm-of-the-Hand Stories

YASUNARI KAWABATA

Translated from the Japanese by

Lane Dunlop and J. Martin Holman

FARRAR, STRAUS AND GIROUX • NEW YORK

Farrar, Straus and Giroux
18 West 18th Street, New York 10011

Printed in the United States of America
Originally published in 1988 by North Point Press
This edition, 2006

Library of Congress Control Number: 2006928261
ISBN-13: 978-0-374-53049-5
ISBN-10: 0-374-53049-1

Designed by Jonathan D. Lippincott

www.fsgbooks.com

7 8 9 10

Contents

Editorial Note

Though known by English readers for his brilliant novelistic work, Yasunari Kawabata believed that the essence of his art was expressed in a series of short short stories written over the entire span of his career. Despite their brevity, these stories contain most of the elements of Kawabata's longer work. Just as a *haiku* may contain a richness rivaling that of a longer poem, so these stories, in the plenitude of their content, the complexity of their psychology, and the sharpness of their observation of human life, rival longer prose fictions. Kawabata said of them, "Many writers, in their youth, write poetry: I, instead of poetry, wrote the palm-of-the-hand stories. Among them are unreasonably fabricated pieces, but there are more than a few good ones that flowed from my pen naturally, of their own accord. . . . [T]he poetic spirit of my young days lives on in them."

Translators' Notes

The origin of my serious interest in Yasunari Kawabata's palm-of-the-hand stories is a letter from Donald Keene, dated January 23, 1982. He had written to me about a childhood memory piece that had appeared the previous year in the *Hudson Review*. He had evidently also seen a not very successful translation by me of an excerpt from Hori Tatsuo's "The Wind Is Rising." The letter went on: "It made me think, after finishing your piece, that you may have been translating the wrong works from Japanese. The vocabulary that you naturally command or, for that matter, your manner of observing things, does not in the least resemble that of Hori Tatsuo. Perhaps you feel a special affinity for the content of his works, but in translating an author with his restricted expression you may be doing yourself a disservice. Who then? Have you read the early works of Kawabata? They are much more experimental than the novels that brought him his Nobel Prize, and I think you might find them more congenial in style."

I had read many of the palm-of-the-hand stories, but hadn't "gotten" most of them. Of those that I read, I had translated and published just three in *Prairie Schooner*, in 1979: "The Grasshopper and the Bell Cricket," "The Silverberry Thief," and "The Young Lady of Suruga." But I had been unable to find any others that reached me or, it would be more accurate to say, that I reached an empathetic understanding of. I mistook their subtlety for slightness, their lack of emphasis for pointlessness.

Their variety also threw me off, since at that time I was looking for a few very particular kinds of stories. So there the matter rested, until time and Professor Keene's remark, germinating in my mind, caused me to return to the palm-of-the-hand stories in the fall of 1986. My experience as I reread the stories reminded me of the biblical phrase about the scales falling from one's eyes. Even those that I did not immediately understand seemed to say, "Translate me." I did, and then they yielded their point.

Yoshimura Teiji, in his excellent short commentary at the back of the Shinchosha edition, mentions that one of the pieces, "Thank You," a mere four pages of sparse dialogue (much of it consisting of repeated "thank you"s), was once made into a movie. That is an indication of the microscopic concision, capable of being magnified with no loss of proportion, of Kawabata's method. Also in the background of such work are the traditional Japanese love of the delicate and the beautiful, the ability to endow a small space with spaciousness, and an exact, X-ray eye for the telling detail, the behavioral clue, although this last quality may be more specifically Kawabata's own. The palm-of-the-hand stories have afforded me a double pleasure: that of living vicariously in another time and place, of escaping myself, as I translated them, and conversely that of getting to know myself a little better as I came to understand them. It is my hope they will provide the reader with a similar pleasure.

Lane Dunlop

Just three months before his death in April 1972, Yasunari Kawabata wrote one of his last works, which was not published until autumn of that year. The story, "Gleanings from Snow Country," is a miniaturization of the novel that brought Kawabata his greatest acclaim. "Gleanings" is not actually a condensation of the whole novel; rather, it consists of a series of scenes—concentrating almost entirely on the man Shimamura and the geisha Komako—lifted almost intact from the first quarter of the novel, the intervening material deleted. *Snow Country*, already a rather spare novel in its full form, is reduced to bare bones as a palm-of-the-hand story. What is lost in detail, however, is at least partially recovered in the intensity of the shortened version.

"Gleanings from Snow Country" is unique. Although they may take up themes and situations that Kawabata dealt with in longer works, the other palm-of-the-hand stories are not excerpts or reductions of novels. Nevertheless, the sense that the stories represent the essence or distillation of a larger world gives them a powerful suggestive quality and links together these thematically disparate miniature works.

Kawabata is known as a novelist in the West because of the recognition he received for *Snow Country*, *The Sound of the Mountain*, *Thousand Cranes*, and other novels translated into Western languages. But Kawabata showed little regard for accepted novelistic form: short stories that were intended to be completed in one magazine installment sometimes grew into full-length works with additions in later issues of the same or even a different magazine; chapters were sometimes added to works that were already considered finished; and many of his completed novels seem to have either no "ending" at all or perhaps several potential ones along the way. The palm-of-the-hand story appears to have been Kawabata's basic unit of composition from which his longer works were built, after the manner of linked-verse poetry, in which discrete verses are joined to form a longer poem, the linkage between each dependent on subtle shifts as the poem continues. Rather than a novelist, Kawabata may have been at heart more of a "palmist"—a writer of palm-of-the-hand stories. He composed the largest number of them in his early years, but no doubt he found the form congenial because he returned to it many times throughout his career, ultimately producing as many as 146 by some counts.

The varied effects of the stories and their thematic diversity demonstrate Kawabata's range perhaps more fully than his better-known, longer works. It is tempting to point to the palm-of-the-hand stories as another successful example of the Japanese penchant for miniaturization; however, the palm-of-the-hand story, as a form, seems to belong to Kawabata alone. His juxtapositions of images scintillates with a unique and succinct perception, and the plots, though diminutive, are intriguing and memorable.

I initially translated a few of the palm-of-the-hand stories over seven years ago at the suggestion of Professor Steven D. Carter when I was a student at Brigham Young University. I wish to thank him for planting the seeds of this project during my senior year and for reading and critiquing what were the first translations of Japanese literature I had ever attempted. In the years since, I have benefitted from the assistance of my friends and colleagues Mariko Okabe, Ikuko Kawahigashi, Yasuko Markley, Yoshiaki Yanagisawa, and Hirofumi Ito, who kindly elucidated difficult (for me) passages and provided cultural information. Finally, I would like to thank my wife, Susan James Holman, who read my translations and, as always, offered invaluable advice, suggestions, and moral support.

J. Martin Holman

Palm-of-the-Hand Stories

A Sunny Place

[1923]

The autumn of my twenty-fourth year, I met a girl at an inn by the seashore. It was the beginning of love.

The girl suddenly lifted her head and hid her face with her kimono sleeve. When I noticed her gesture, I thought that I must have displayed my bad habit again. I was embarrassed and made a pained expression.

"I stare at you, don't I?"

"Yes . . . but it's not that." Her voice was gentle and her words lighthearted. I felt relieved.

"It bothers you, doesn't it?"

"No. It's all right, but . . . really, it's all right."

She lowered her sleeve. Her expression showed the effort she had to make to allow herself to be seen. Turning away, I looked toward the ocean.

I have long had a habit of staring at people who sit beside me. I had often thought to cure myself of this habit, but I found it painful not to look into the faces of those around me. I felt an intense self-hatred every time I realized I was doing it. Maybe this habit came from having spent all my time reading others' faces once I had lost my parents and my home when I was a child and gone to live with others. Perhaps that is why I've turned out this way, I thought.

At one point I tried to determine whether this habit had developed after I was taken in by others or whether I had had it before that, when I was in my own home. But I could find no recollection that would make this clear to me.

Anyway, as I turned my eyes away from the girl, I noticed a sunny place on the beach suffused with the autumn sunlight. That sunny place called up a long-buried memory.

After my parents died, I had lived alone with my grandfather for almost ten years in a house in the country. My grandfather was blind. For years he sat in the same room, in the same spot, facing the east with a long charcoal brazier in front of him. Occasionally he would turn his head toward the south, but he never faced the north. Once I became aware of my grandfather's habit of turning to face only one direction, I became terribly concerned. Sometimes I would sit for a long time in front of my grandfather staring into his face, wondering if he would turn to the north even once. But my grandfather would turn his head to the right every five minutes like an electrical doll, looking only toward the south. It gave me a sad feeling. It seemed uncanny. But to the south was a sunny place; I wondered if the south felt ever so slightly lighter even to a blind person.

Now, looking at the beach I recalled that other sunny place I had forgotten.

In those days, I had stared at my grandfather's face, wanting him to face north. Since he was blind, I often stared fixedly at him. That had developed into my habit of watching peoples' faces, I now realized. So my habit had been with me since I was in my own home. It did not spring from base motives. I could feel secure pitying myself for having this habit. Thinking so made me want to jump for joy—all the more because my heart was filled with the desire to cleanse myself for the girl.

The girl spoke again. "I'm used to it, but I'm still a bit shy."

Her words implied that I could return my gaze to her face. She must have been thinking that I had shown bad manners earlier.

I looked at her, my face brighter. She blushed and gave me a sly glance. "My face will become less and less novel with each day and night. So I'm not worried." She spoke like a child.

I smiled. I felt as if a kind of intimacy had suddenly been added to our relationship. I wanted to go out to the sunny place on the beach, carrying with me the memory of the girl and my grandfather.

JMH

The Weaker Vessel

[1924]

At a corner in the town was a curio shop. And between the road and the front of the shop stood a ceramic statue of the Buddhist deity Kannon. The statue was about the size of a twelve-year-old girl. When the train went by, the cold skin of the Kannon shivered slightly, along with the glass door of the shop. Every time I passed by the shop, I worried that the statue might tumble into the road. So this is the dream I had:

The Kannon's body was falling directly toward me.

The Kannon suddenly thrust out its long, ample, white arm and wrapped it around my neck. I sprang back—from the uncanniness of its inanimate arm alone coming to life and the cold touch of ceramic skin.

Without a sound, the Kannon shattered to bits beside the road.

A girl picked up some of the pieces. She stooped a bit, hurriedly gathering the scattered, glittering ceramic shards. I was startled to see her appear. As I opened my mouth to offer some excuse, I woke up.

It had all seemed to happen in the instant after the Kannon had fallen.

I tried to interpret this dream.

"Give honor unto the wife as unto the weaker vessel"—this

verse from the Bible often came to mind back then. I always associated the words "weaker vessel" with a porcelain vessel. And, further, I associated them with the girl in the dream.

A young girl falls easily. In one sense, loving is in itself the falling of a young girl. That is what I thought.

And so, in my dream, might not the girl have been hurriedly gathering the shards of her own fall?

JMH

The Girl Who Approached the Fire

[1924]

The water of the lake glittered in the distance. It was the color of a stagnant spring in an old garden on a moonlit evening.

The woods on the far bank of the lake were burning silently. The flames spread as I watched—a forest fire.

The fire truck hurrying along the bank like a toy was reflected vividly on the surface of the water. Crowds of people blackened the hill, endlessly streaming up the slope from below.

When I came to myself, the air around me was still and bright, as though dry.

The strip of town at the base of the slope was a sea of fire.

A girl parted the crowd of people and descended the slope alone. She was the only one going down the hill.

Strangely, it was a world without sound.

When I saw the girl walking directly toward the sea of fire, I could not bear it.

Then, without words, I actually conversed with her feelings.

"Why are you going down the hill alone? Is it to die by fire?"

"I don't want to die, but your home lies to the west and so I am going east."

The sight of her—a dark spot against the flames that filled my vision—pierced my eyes. I woke up.

There were tears in the corners of my eyes.

She had said that she did not want to go in the direction of my house. I already understood that. Whatever she thought was all right. Forcing myself to be rational, on the surface I had resigned myself that her feelings toward me had cooled; nevertheless, quite willfully I wanted to imagine, unconnected with the actual girl herself, that somewhere in her emotions she had a drop of feeling for me. Even as I sneered at this self, I secretly wanted to bring it to life.

However, did this dream mean that I believed in the depths of my heart that she had not the least affection for me?

The dream was an expression of my emotions. And her emotions in the dream were those I had created for her. They were mine. In a dream there is no bluffing or pretense.

I felt desolate to think so.

JMH

A Saw and Childbirth

[1924]

What did it mean? Well, anyway, I understood that it was Italy. On the top of the hill stood a tent that looked like a striped parasol. The flag on top of it fluttered in the May ocean breeze. Below the green forest was the blue sea. (It reminded me of the coast near a mountain hot spring in Izu.) Inside the tent was something that looked like a telephone booth. It also resembled a steamship-ticket sales office or a customs office, but actually all I did there was to receive a vast amount of exchange money from the window. A packet wrapped in yellow paper slapped the palm of my left hand. I felt the money inside. A woman in a plain black dress stood beside me. She started to speak. Though I realized she was a Japanese woman, I looked at her thinking that I did not understand Italian.

Then what happened? The setting changed to the farming village that was my hometown.

There were ten people gathered in the garden of a farmhouse with a splendid gate. They were all people I knew from the village, but when I woke up I could not remember who they were. Anyway, for some reason, the woman and I had come to a duel.

Before going out to the battlefield, I wanted to urinate. Since people were watching, I stood there flustered, with my hand on my kimono, not knowing what to do. When I looked back suddenly, I saw that I was fighting with the woman, flashing a white sword in the middle of the garden. Although I knew it was a dream, I was startled to see myself.

"If you see your own illusion, your own self, your own second personality, you will die."

I felt as though my second self was going to be cut down by the woman. Her weapon looked like a saw. It was a sword that was shaped like a wide saw such as a lumberjack would use to cut down huge trees.

At some point, I forgot about urinating. I became one with my second self and was locked in battle with the woman. Her weapon looked like a bright ornament, and every time my sword bit into hers, her weapon became nicked and dented. Finally it turned into a real saw. These words sounded clearly in my ears.

"This is how the saw came to be."

In other words, it was odd because this battle represented the invention of the saw. It was indeed a battle, but I slashed and cut with the sensation that I was just absentmindedly watching a fight scene in a movie.

Finally, I plopped down in the middle of the garden. Catching hold of her saw between the soles of my feet, I teased the woman. She was unable to push or pull the saw.

"I'm weak because I just had a baby."

Indeed, how ample were the folds that hung from her belly!

Next I was scampering along a road that had been cut through the rocks by the coast. (It looked like the beach at Yuzaki on the Kii Peninsula.) I could sense that I was running to see her baby. The newborn baby was sleeping inside a cave at the tip of the promontory. The smell of the surf was like a green light.

The woman smiled beautifully. "Giving birth to a baby is nothing at all."

I felt a glowing joy as I held the woman's shoulders. "Let's tell her, shall we? Let's tell her," I said.

"Yes, let's tell her that having a baby is nothing at all."

Now the woman had become two people. The woman I was talking to was saying she would tell the other woman, who was somewhere else.

Then I woke up. I have not seen the woman in my dream for five years. I do not even know where she is. The thought that she might have borne a child had never even crossed my mind. But I felt that this dream hinted at the relationship between the woman and me.

While I lay in bed, I went over the dream again, enjoying the refreshing delight it had left in my head. Somewhere would she bear someone's child?

JMH

The Grasshopper and the Bell Cricket

[1924]

Walking along the tile-roofed wall of the university, I turned aside and approached the upper school. Behind the white board fence of the school playground, from a dusky clump of bushes under the black cherry trees, an insect's voice could be heard. Walking more slowly and listening to that voice, and feeling reluctant to part with it, I turned right so as not to leave the playground behind. When I turned to the left, the fence gave way to an embankment planted with orange trees. At the corner, I exclaimed with surprise. My eyes gleaming at what they saw up ahead, I hurried forward with short steps.

At the base of the embankment was a bobbing cluster of beautiful varicolored lanterns, such as one might see at a festival in a remote country village. Without going any farther, I knew that it was a group of children on an insect chase among the bushes of the embankment. There were about twenty lanterns. Not only were there crimson, pink, indigo, green, purple, and yellow lanterns, but one lantern glowed with five colors at once. There were even some little red store-bought lanterns. But most of the lanterns were beautiful square ones that the children had made themselves with love and care. The bobbing lanterns, the coming together of children on this lonely slope—surely it was a scene from a fairy tale?

One of the neighborhood children had heard an insect sing on this slope one night. Buying a red lantern, he had come back the next night to find the insect. The night after that, there was another child. This new child could not buy a lantern. Cutting out the back and front of a small carton and papering it, he placed a candle on the bottom and fastened a string to the top. The number of children grew to five, and then to seven. They learned how to color the paper that they stretched over the windows of the cutout cartons, and to draw pictures on it. Then these wise child-artists, cutting out round, three-cornered, and lozenge leaf shapes in the cartons, coloring each little window a different color, with circles and diamonds, red and green, made a single and whole decorative pattern. The child with the red lantern discarded it as a tasteless object that could be bought at a store. The child who had made his own lantern threw it away because the design was too simple. The pattern of light that one had had in hand the night before was unsatisfying the morning after. Each day, with cardboard, paper, brush, scissors, penknife, and glue, the children made new lanterns out of their hearts and minds. Look at my lantern! Be the most unusually beautiful! And each night, they had gone out on their insect hunts. These were the twenty children and their beautiful lanterns that I now saw before me.

Wide-eyed, I loitered near them. Not only did the square lanterns have old-fashioned patterns and flower shapes, but the names of the children who had made them were cut in squared letters of the syllabary. Different from the painted-over red lanterns, others (made of thick cut-out cardboard) had their designs drawn onto the paper windows, so that the candle's light seemed to emanate from the form and color of the design itself. The lanterns brought out the shadows of the bushes like dark light. The children crouched eagerly on the slope wherever they heard an insect's voice.

"Does anyone want a grasshopper?" A boy, who had been peering into a bush about thirty feet away from the other children, suddenly straightened up and shouted.

"Yes! Give it to me!" Six or seven children came running up. Crowding behind the boy who had found the grasshopper, they peered into the bush. Brushing away their outstretched hands and spreading out his arms, the boy stood as if guarding the bush where the insect was. Waving the lantern in his right hand, he called again to the other children.

"Does anyone want a grasshopper? A grasshopper!"

"I do! I do!" Four or five more children came running up. It seemed you could not catch a more precious insect than a grasshopper. The boy called out a third time.

"Doesn't anyone want a grasshopper?"

Two or three more children came over.

"Yes. I want it."

It was a girl, who just now had come up behind the boy who'd discovered the insect. Lightly turning his body, the boy gracefully bent forward. Shifting the lantern to his left hand, he reached his right hand into the bush.

"It's a grasshopper."

"Yes. I'd like to have it."

The boy quickly stood up. As if to say "Here!" he thrust out his fist that held the insect at the girl. She, slipping her left wrist under the string of her lantern, enclosed the boy's fist with both hands. The boy quietly opened his fist. The insect was transfered to between the girl's thumb and index finger.

"Oh! It's not a grasshopper. It's a bell cricket." The girl's eyes shone as she looked at the small brown insect.

"It's a bell cricket! It's a bell cricket!" the children echoed in an envious chorus.

"It's a bell cricket. It's a bell cricket."

Glancing with her bright intelligent eyes at the boy who had given her the cricket, the girl opened the little insect cage hanging at her side and released the cricket in it.

"It's a bell cricket."

"Oh, it's a bell cricket," the boy who'd captured it muttered. Holding up the insect cage close to his eyes, he looked inside it. By the light of his beautiful many-colored lantern, also held up at eye level, he glanced at the girl's face.

Oh, I thought. I felt slightly jealous of the boy, and sheepish. How silly of me not to have understood his actions until now! Then I caught my breath in surprise. Look! It was something on the girl's breast that neither the boy who had given her the cricket, nor she who had accepted it, nor the children who were looking at them noticed.

In the faint greenish light that fell on the girl's breast, wasn't the name "Fujio" clearly discernible? The boy's lantern, which he held up alongside the girl's insect cage, inscribed his name, cut out in the green papered aperture, onto her white cotton kimono. The girl's lantern, which dangled loosely from her wrist, did not project its pattern so clearly, but still one could make out, in a trembling patch of red on the boy's waist, the name "Kiyoko." This chance interplay of red and green—if it was chance or play—neither Fujio nor Kiyoko knew about.

Even if they remembered forever that Fujio had given her the cricket and that Kiyoko had accepted it, not even in dreams would Fujio ever know that his name had been written in green on Kiyoko's breast or that Kiyoko's name had been inscribed in red on his waist, nor would Kiyoko ever know that Fujio's name had been inscribed in green on her breast or that her own name had been written in red on Fujio's waist.

Fujio! Even when you have become a young man, laugh with pleasure at a girl's delight when, told that it's a grasshopper, she is given a bell cricket; laugh with affection at a girl's chagrin when, told that it's a bell cricket, she is given a grasshopper.

Even if you have the wit to look by yourself in a bush away from the other children, there are not many bell crickets in the world. Probably you will find a girl like a grasshopper whom you think is a bell cricket.

And finally, to your clouded, wounded heart, even a true bell cricket will seem like a grasshopper. Should that day come, when it seems to you that the world is only full of grasshoppers, I will think it a pity that you have no way to remember tonight's play of light, when your name was written in green by your beautiful lantern on a girl's breast.

LD

The Ring

[1924]

An impecunious law student, taking some translation work with him, went to a mountain hot-spring inn.

Three geisha from the city, holding their round fans to their faces, were napping in the little pavilion in the forest.

He descended the stone stairs at the edge of the forest to the mountain stream. A great boulder divided the current of the stream; swarms of dragonflies hovered and darted there.

A girl was standing naked by the bathtub that had been carved out of the boulder.

Thinking she was eleven or twelve, he ignored her as he shed his bathrobe on the beach and lowered himself into the tub at the girl's feet.

The girl, who seemed to have nothing else to do, smiled at him, showing herself off, as if to attract him to her rosy pink body. A split-second glance at her told him that she was the child of a geisha. Hers was an abnormal, precocious beauty, in which one could sense her future purpose of giving sensual pleasure to men. His eyes, surprised, widened like a fan in their appreciation of her.

Suddenly, the girl, holding up her left hand, gave a small scream.

"Ah! I forgot to take it off. I went in with it on."

Allured despite himself, he looked up at her hand.

"Little brat!" Instead of being irritated at having been taken in by the girl, he suddenly felt a violent dislike for her.

She'd wanted to show off her ring. He didn't know whether one took off one's ring or not when one entered a hot-spring bath, but it was clear that he'd been caught by the child's stratagem.

Evidently, he had shown his displeasure in his face more strongly than he'd thought. The girl, turning red, fiddled with her ring. Hiding his own childishness with a wry smile, he said casually, "That's a nice ring. Let's have a look at it."

"It's an opal."

Sure enough, as if very happy to show it to him, the girl squatted at the edge of the tub. Losing her balance as she held out the hand with the ring on it, she put her other hand on his shoulder.

"An opal?" Receiving an intense impression of her precocity from her pronunciation of the word, he tried repeating it.

"Yes. My finger's still too small. I had the ring made specially of gold. But now people say the stone's too big."

He toyed with the girl's little hand. The stone, a gentle, luminous, warm egg-yolk color suffused with violet, seemed extraordinarily beautiful. The girl, bringing her body straight forward, closer and closer, and gazing into his face, seemed beside herself with satisfaction.

This girl, in order to show him the ring better, might not be surprised even if he took her, all naked as she was, onto his lap.

LD

Hair

[1924]

A girl thought she would have her hair done.

This happened in a little village deep in the mountains.

When she got to the hairdresser's house, the girl was surprised. All the girls of the village had gathered there.

That evening, when the girls' unshapely "cleft-peach" coiffures had all been newly done up, a company of soldiers arrived in the village. They were billeted in the houses by the village office. There was a guest in every single house in the village. Guests were a very rare occurrence; that may have been why all the girls of the village decided to have their hair done.

Of course, nothing happened between the girls and the soldiers. The next morning, the company left the village and crossed over the mountain.

However, the exhausted hairdresser thought she would take the next four days off. With the pleasant feeling that comes after hard work, on the same morning as the soldiers and over the same mountain, she joggled to and fro in the horse-drawn wagon as she went to visit her man.

When she arrived at the slightly larger village on the other side of the mountain, the hairdresser there said to her, "I'm so happy. You've come at just the right time. Please help me out a little."

Here, also, the girls of the mountainside had all gathered to have their hair done.

Working all that day again on cleft-peach hairdos, she set

out in the evening for the little silver mine where her man worked. As soon as she saw him, the hairdresser said, "If I followed the soldiers around, I do believe I'd become a rich woman."

"By tagging around after soldiers? Don't make bad jokes. Those young whippersnappers in their yellow-brown uniforms? You fool."

The man gave the hairdresser a whack.

With a sweet feeling, as if her dead-tired body had gone numb, the woman glared at the man.

A bugle call, clear and full of strength, from the company that had crossed the mountain and was marching down toward them, echoed through the village twilight.

LD

Canaries

[1924]

Madam:

I must break my promise and write a letter to you just one more time.

I can no longer keep the canaries I received from you last year. My wife always cared for them. My only function was to look at them—to think of you when I saw them.

You were the one who said it, weren't you? "You have a wife and I have a husband. Let's stop seeing each other. If only you didn't have a wife. I am giving you these canaries to remember me by. Look at them. These canaries are a couple now, but the shopkeeper simply caught a male and a female at random and put them in a cage. The canaries themselves had nothing to do with it. Anyway, please remember me with these birds. Perhaps it's odd to give living creatures as a souvenir, but our memories, too, are alive. Someday the canaries will die. And, when the time comes that the memories between us must die, let them die."

Now the canaries look as though they are about to die. The one who kept them has died. A painter like me, negligent and poor as I am, cannot keep such frail birds. I'll put it plainly. My wife used to care for the birds, and now she is dead. Since my wife has died, I wonder if the birds will also die. And so, madam, was it my wife who brought me memories of you?

I considered setting the canaries free, but, since my wife's death, the birds' wings appear to have suddenly grown weak.

Besides, these birds don't know the sky. This pair has no companions in the city or woods nearby with whom they could flock. And if one of them were to fly off alone, they would each die separately. But, then, you *did* say that the man at the pet shop had merely caught one male and one female at random and put them in a cage.

Speaking of which, I don't want to sell them back to a bird dealer because you gave these birds to me. And I don't want to return them to you either, since my wife was the one who cared for them. Besides, these birds—which you had probably already forgotten—would be a lot of trouble for you.

I'll say it again. It was because my wife was here that the birds have lived until now—serving as a memory of you. So, madam, I want to have the canaries follow her in death. Keeping my memories of you alive was not the only thing my wife did. How was I able to have loved a woman like you? Wasn't it because my wife remained with me? My wife made me forget all the pain in my life. She avoided seeing the other half of my life. Had she not done so, I would surely have averted my eyes or cast down my gaze before a woman like you.

Madam, it's all right, isn't it, if I kill the canaries and bury them in my wife's grave?

JMH

Harbor Town

[1924]

This harbor town is an interesting one.

Respectable housewives and girls come to the inn, and, as long as a guest is there, one of the women will stay overnight with him. From the time he gets up, at lunch and on walks, she is at his side. They're just like a couple on their honeymoon.

Yet, when he says that he will take her to a nearby hot-spring inn, the woman will tilt her head and think. However, when he says he will rent a house in this town, she, if she is a young woman, will most likely say happily, "I'll be your wife. As long as it's not for too long. As long as it's not for a year or even for half a year."

That morning, the man was hurriedly packing his things in preparation for his departure by boat. The woman, as she helped him, said, "Won't you write a letter for me?"

"What? Now?"

"But I'm not your wife anymore, so it's all right. All the time you were here, I was by your side, wasn't I? I didn't do anything bad. But now I'm not your wife anymore."

"Is that so—is that so?" He wrote the letter to the man for her. It was evidently a man who, like himself, had spent half a month with this woman at the inn.

"Won't you send me a letter, too? On a morning when some other man is boarding the boat? When you're no longer his wife?"

LD

Photograph

[1924]

An ugly man—it's rude to say so, but it was surely because of his ugliness that he had become a poet—this poet told me the following:

"I hate photographs, and I rarely think of having one taken. The only time was about four or five years ago with a girl on the occasion of our engagement. She was very dear to me; I have no confidence that such a woman will appear again in my lifetime. Now those photographs are my one beautiful memory.

"Anyway, last year a magazine wanted to carry a photograph of me. I cut my picture out of a photograph that I had had taken of myself with my fiancée and her sister and sent it to the magazine. Recently, a newspaper reporter came asking for my picture. I thought for a moment. Then finally I cut a picture of my fiancée and myself in half and gave it to the reporter. I told him to make sure to return it, but I don't think I'll ever get it back. Well, it doesn't matter.

"I say it doesn't matter, but still, I was quite startled when I looked at this half of a photograph where my fiancée had been left alone. Was this the same girl? Let me tell you about her.

"The girl in the picture was beautiful and charming. She was seventeen then and in love. But when I looked at the photograph I had in my hand—this photograph of the girl severed from me—I realized what a dull girl she was. And until that moment it had been the most beautiful photograph I'd ever seen. . . . But in an instant I awoke from a long dream. My precious treasure crumbled. And so . . ."

The poet lowered his voice still more.

"If she sees my picture in the paper, surely she will think so too. She will be mortified that she loved a man like me even for a moment.

"Well, that's the story.

"But, I wonder, if the newspaper were to carry that picture of the two of us together, as it was taken, would she come running back to me thinking what a fine man I was?"

JMH

The White Flower

[1924]

Marriages of blood relatives had continued through the generations until the girl's family had gradually died out from lung disease. She, too, was rather small in the shoulders. Men were probably startled when they embraced her.

A kind woman once told her, "Take care in marriage. It wouldn't do to have someone too strong. A man who looks weak, with no diseases and a fair complexion, would be all right. . . . Just so he has no history of lung disease. Someone who always sits properly, doesn't drink, and smiles a lot."

The girl, however, enjoyed daydreaming of a strong man's arms—strong arms that would make her ribs crack when they were wrapped around her. For, although her face looked relaxed, she felt desperate. When she closed her eyes, she saw her body floating on the ocean of life, drifting wherever the tide took it. This gave her an amorous air.

A letter came from her cousin. "My chest is finally giving me trouble. I can only say that the time of my fate, to which I have resigned myself, has come. I am calm. However, there is one vexing part. Why, while I was still healthy, did I not once ask you to let me kiss you? Please don't let your lips be sullied by this germ."

She hurried to her cousin's home. Soon she was sent to a sanatorium near the seashore.

The young doctor cared for her as if she were his only patient. He carried her cloth lounge chair like a cradle out to the end of the cape every day. There, the bamboo grove always glistened in the sunlight.

It was sunrise.

"Ah, you've recovered completely—really, completely. How I've waited for this day." The doctor picked her up from the lounge which was set up on the rock. "Your life is rising anew like that sun. Why don't the ships at sea hoist pink sails for you? I hope you will forgive me. I've waited for this day with two hearts—as the doctor who has cured you and also as my other self. How I've longed for today! How painful it's been that I couldn't throw off my doctor's conscience. You're perfectly well. You're well enough that you can use your body to express your emotions. . . . Why doesn't the whole ocean turn pink for us?"

Full of gratitude, the girl looked up at the doctor. Then she shifted her eyes to the sea and waited.

But suddenly she was startled by the realization that she had no thought of chastity. She had foreseen her own death from her childhood, so she did not believe in time; she did not believe in the continuation of time. And so it would be impossible to be chaste.

"How often I've gazed at your body in an emotional way. But I've also gazed at your body all over in a rational way. To me, as a doctor, your body was a laboratory."

"What?"

"A beautiful laboratory. If medicine weren't my calling from heaven, my emotions would have killed you by now."

She began to feel hatred toward the doctor. She changed her position in order to avoid his eyes.

A young novelist who was a patient in the same hospital spoke to her. "We should congratulate each other. Let's leave the hospital on the same day."

The two of them got into a car at the gate and drove through a pine grove.

The novelist started to put his arm around the woman's shoulders. She began to lean against him as though she were a light object, falling, with no power to stop herself.

The two went on a trip.

"This is the pink dawn of life—your morning and my morning. How strange it is to have two mornings in this world at the same time. The two mornings will become one. That's good. I'll write a book called *Two Mornings*."

Filled with joy, she looked up at the novelist.

"Look at this. It's a sketch I made of you while in the hospital. Even if you and I were to die, we might live in my novel. But now there are two mornings—the transparent beauty of characteristics that are no characteristics at all. You bring a beauty like a fragrance that you can't see with the naked eye, like the pollen that perfumes the spring fields. My novel has found a beautiful soul. How shall I write it? Put your soul in the palm of my hand for me to look at, like a crystal jewel. I'll sketch it in words. . . ."

"What?"

"With such beautiful material—if I weren't a novelist, my emotions could not have let you live into the distant future."

Then she began to feel hatred toward the novelist. She straightened herself up to avoid his gaze.

She sat alone in her own room. Her cousin had died a little earlier.

"Pink, pink."

As she peered up at her white skin that gradually grew limpid, she recalled the word "pink" and smiled.

"If some man would woo me with one word . . . ," she felt like nodding. And she smiled.

JMH

The Incident of the Dead Face

[1925]

"Please come see her. This is what's become of her. Oh, how she wanted to see you once more." The man's mother-in-law spoke as she hurriedly led him to the room. The people at his wife's bedside all looked toward him at the same time.

"Please take a look at her." His wife's mother spoke again as she started to remove the cloth covering his wife's face.

Then he spoke suddenly, in spite of himself. "Just a moment. Could I see her alone? Could you leave me alone with her here in the room?"

His words aroused sympathy in his wife's family. They quietly left, closing the sliding partition behind them.

He removed the white cloth.

His wife's face had stiffened into a pained expression in death. Her cheeks were hollow and her discolored teeth protruded from between her lips. The flesh of her eyelids was withered and clung to her eyeballs. An obvious tension had frozen the pain in her forehead.

He sat still for a moment, staring down at this ugly dead face.

Then, he placed his trembling hands on his wife's lips and tried to close her mouth. He forced her lips shut, but they fell open limply when he released his hands. He closed her mouth again. Again it opened. He did the same thing over and over, but the only result was that the hard lines around his wife's mouth began to soften.

Then he felt a growing passion in his fingertips. He rubbed her forehead to try to relieve its look of grim anxiety. His palms grew hot.

Once more he sat still, looking down at the new face.

His wife's mother and younger sister came in. "You're probably tired from the train ride. Please have some lunch and take a rest. . . . Oh!" Tears suddenly trickled down the mother's cheeks. "The human spirit is a frightening thing. She couldn't die completely until you came back. It's so strange. All you did was take one look at her and her face became so relaxed. . . . It's all right. Now she's all right."

His wife's younger sister, her eyes clear with an unearthly beauty, looked into his eyes, which were tinged with madness. Then she, too, burst into tears.

JMH

Glass

[1925]

His fifteen-year-old fiancée Yōko lost the color in her cheeks and returned home. "I have a headache. I saw something so pitiful."

A young worker at a glass factory that made sake bottles had spit up blood, then had burned himself severely and lost consciousness. She had seen it happen.

Her fiancé also knew of the glass factory. Since it was hot work, the windows were open almost all year long. There were always two or three passersby standing at the windows. The stream across the street did not flow. The oil on it glistened. It was like a decaying sewer.

Inside the damp factory, where the sun did not shine, the workers brandished balls of fire on long poles. Sweat poured from their shirts as it did from their faces, and their faces were as soiled as their shirts. The ball of fire at the end of the pole would begin to stretch into the shape of a bottle. They would put it in water, then lift it out after a while and break it off with a snap. A bent-backed little urchin would pick it up with tongs, then run it to the finishing furnace. Within ten minutes the people who stopped to watch at the factory windows would have their heads roughened and hardened like a shard of glass by the excitement and the sound of the flying balls of fire and glass.

While Yōko was peeking in, a boy who was carrying a bottle spit up thick blood and fell exhausted to the floor, his hands over his mouth. Then a flying ball of fire struck his shoulder, and he opened his blood-covered mouth and screamed as if he would split in two. Jumping up, he ran around once, then fell to the floor.

"Watch out, you idiot!"

They put some water on his shoulder. The young worker was unconscious.

"He surely doesn't have money to go to the hospital. I want to go visit him," she told her fiancé.

"Then you should. But he's not the only worker who needs pity, you know."

"Yes. Thank you. That makes me happy."

Twenty days later, the young laborer came to thank the girl for the visit. He wanted to speak to the "young miss," so Yōko came out to the entryway. The young man was standing in the garden. When she appeared, he held on to the door frame and bowed his head.

"Well, are you better now?"

"What?" The pale boy was startled. Yōko looked as though she would cry.

"Is your burn all right now?"

"Yeah." The boy started to unbutton his shirt.

"No, that's all right . . ."

Yōko ran inside the room and started to speak to her fiancé. "I . . ." Her fiancé gave her some money.

"Give this to him."

"I don't want to go. Please have the maid do it."

Ten years later.

The man read a story called "Glass" in a literary magazine. It described their neighborhood. There was a stream that did not flow, with oil that glistened on its surface. There was a hell where balls of fire flew. Spitting blood. A burn. The blessing from a bourgeois girl.

"Hey, Yōko. Yōko!"

"What is it?"

"You once saw a boy in a glass factory faint, and you gave him money, didn't you? When you were a first- or second-year student at the girls' school?"

"Yes. Yes, I did."

"That boy has become a writer—and he wrote about that."

"What? Let me see."

Yōko grabbed the magazine from him. But, as he read further over his wife's shoulder, he began to regret having shown the story to her.

It said that later the boy had gone to work in a flower-vase factory. There he showed great talent at designing the color and shape of the vases, so he did not have to drive his sick body as harshly as he had done before. It also said that he had sent the girl the most beautiful vase he had ever designed.

"No, for four or five years"—this is the gist of what he wrote—"I made vases unceasingly with the bourgeois girl as my inspiration. Was it my miserable labor experiences that awakened me to a sense of social class? Or was it my love for the bourgeois girl? It would have been most appropriate to have coughed up blood then—to have coughed up all my blood and died. The blessing of a haunting enemy. The humiliation. Long ago, the daughter of a warrior whose castle was taken was saved by the pity of the enemy; nevertheless, the daughter suffered the fate of becoming the concubine of the man who killed her father. The first blessing from the girl was that she saved my life. The second was that she gave me the opportunity to look for a new job. But consider my new job—which class was I making vases for? I had become the concubine of my enemy. I realized how that girl could be so lovely; I knew why I had been blessed. But, just as a man cannot walk on four legs like a lion, I could not wash away the dream of the girl. I imagined that my enemy's house was burning down, and I could hear her lamentations as the beautiful vase in her gay room crumbled into ugliness. I imagined the girl's beauty being destroyed. Though I stood on the battlefront of the classes, I was, in the long run, only a single pane of glass. A single lump of glass. Still, in these modern times, is there even one among us who does not feel the glass on his back? First, we must make our enemies break the glass on our backs. If we vanish with the glass, it cannot be helped, but, if we are relieved of our burden, we shall dance and continue the battle."

After reading the story, Yōko looked as if she were considering something in the distance. "I wonder where that vase went."

He had never seen such a meek face on his wife.

"But I was a child then."

His color changed. "That's right. Whether you fight with another class or even take the position of another class and fight with your own, first of all, you must recognize that you will soon be destroyed as an individual."

But this was odd. The man had never once in all these years felt the loveliness and freshness in his wife that he perceived in the girl in the story.

How could that bent-backed, pale, sick urchin have this kind of power?

JMH

The O-Shin Jizō

[1925]

In the back garden of the hot-spring inn, there was a big chestnut tree. The O-Shin Jizō, a statue of the guardian of children put up in the lady's name, stood underneath the tree.

According to the tourist's guidebook for the area, O-Shin had died in the fifth year of Meiji, at the age of sixty-three. After her husband had died when she was twenty-four, she had not remarried, but all the young men of the village, without a single exception, had come to her bed. O-Shin had accorded the same welcome to all of them. The young men, establishing an order of visitation among themselves, had shared O-Shin. When a boy reached a certain age, he was received by the young men into the company of co-possessors of O-Shin. When a young man took a wife, he was obliged to withdraw from that company. Thanks to O-Shin, the young men of the mountain did not have to travel beyond the mountain pass to the women of the harbor town, the virgins of the mountain had remained virgins, and the wives of the mountain had remained faithful. Just as all the men of this mountain valley had to cross the hanging bridge to reach their different hamlets, so all the young men of this hamlet entered their adult lives by frequenting O-Shin.

The guest thought this legend beautiful. He felt a yearning for O-Shin. But the O-Shin Jizō did not look like O-Shin. It had a priest's tonsured head, and one could scarcely make out the eyes and nose on its face. Perhaps somebody had picked up an old Jizō that had fallen over in the cemetery and brought it here.

Across from the chestnut tree, there was a house of pleasure. The bathing guests, sneaking over there from the inn, would stroke the bald head of the O-Shin Jizō each time they passed beneath the chestnut tree.

One day in summer, the guest sat with three or four others who were sucking on shaved ice. He took a mouthful and, frowning, immediately spat it out.

"Is something wrong with it?" one of the chambermaids asked.

He pointed toward the brothel beyond the chestnut tree.

"You probably got it from that place."

"Yes."

"One of the women over there must have shaved it. It's unclean, isn't it?"

"What a thing to say! The madam herself shaved it. I saw her when I went to get it."

"But the women must have washed the glasses and the spoons."

Putting aside the glass as if throwing it away, he spat out his saliva.

On his way back from viewing the falls, he stopped a horse-drawn bus. As he got on, he stiffened. A girl of unusual beauty was riding on the bus. The more he looked at this girl, the more he felt the woman in her. The fresh, warm desires of the brothel, soaking into the girl's body since she was a baby of three, must have steeped her flesh in the wetness of love. Nowhere in the rounded curves of her body was there a place that jarred the eye. Even the soles of her feet were not thick. Her flat face, in which the black eyes opened startlingly, gave off a sort of fresh and untiring absentmindedness. Her smooth, glossy skin—one could tell the color of her legs from a glance at her cheeks—made one want to tread on her barefoot. She was a soft, conscienceless bed. This woman had been born to make men forget their scruples.

Growing warm at the sight of her knees, he turned away and looked at distant Mount Fuji, which floated above the valley. After a while, looking back and forth between the mountain and the girl, he began to feel the beauty of carnal passion.

Accompanied by an old country woman, the girl got off when he did. She crossed the hanging bridge and descended into the valley. She entered the house beyond the chestnut tree. He was surprised, but he felt a beautiful satisfaction at the fate of this girl.

"This woman, no matter how many men she knows, will never grow weary or dissolute. This born prostitute, unlike the common prostitutes of the world, will never lose the color of her skin and eyes, will never lose the shape of her neck and bosom and waist."

He grew tearful with the joy of having found a holy person. He had seen the features of O-Shin, he thought.

That autumn, unable to wait for the hunting season to start, he came again to the mountain inn.

The guests had gone out into the back garden. The cook was beating the branches of the chestnut tree with a stick. The autumn-colored burrs fell to the ground. The women, picking them up, peeled them.

"Fine. Let me test my marksmanship."

Taking his rifle from its carrying case, he took aim at the treetop. Before the shot echoed back from the valley, the chestnut burrs came showering down. The women gave a shout of victory. The inn's hunting dog leapt up at the report of the gun.

He looked past the tree. That girl was walking toward him. Although her fine-grained skin was still beautiful, there was a sunken pallor about it now. He turned to the women at his side.

"That person has been sick in bed for a long time."

He felt a forlorn disillusionment toward the thing called carnal passion. Feeling confused and indignant, he pulled the trigger several times in succession.

Shots shattered the autumn calm of the mountain. Chestnuts rained down.

The dog ran toward the downed chestnuts. Howling playfully, he lowered his head and stretched out his front paws. Lightly batting at the burrs, he howled again. The pale-faced girl said, "Ah, the burrs are painful even to the dog's feet."

The women burst out laughing. The autumn sky arched high overhead. One more shot.

A drop of that brown autumn rain, a chestnut burr fell right on top of the bald priest's head of the O-Shin Jizō. The burr flew to pieces. The women, laughing as if they would fall apart, shouted with victory.

LD

The Sliding Rock

[1925]

With his wife and child, he had come to the mountain hot spring. It was a famous hot spring, said to induce fertility. Its waters were extraordinarily hot, so doubtless it was good for women. In addition, superstition had it that a certain nearby pine tree and rock used to bestow children on the bathers.

As he was being shaved by the barber, who had a face like a pickled cucumber seasoned in sake lees, he asked about the pine tree. (In recording this story, I must be careful to preserve the good name of womankind.)

"When I was a boy, we often went to look at the women. We'd get up before dawn to see them wrap themselves around the pine tree. Anyhow, women who want children go crazy."

"Can you still see them do that?"

"Well, now, the tree was cut down ten years ago. Anyhow, it was a great big tree. They built two houses with the lumber."

"Hmm, but who cut it down? The person who cut it down must have been quite a guy."

"Well, now, it was an order from the prefectural office. Anyhow, the good old days are gone forever."

Before supper, he and his wife soaked themselves in the Great Spring, so called because, although it was communal, it was the one said to work for women and thus was the jewel of the establishment. It was the custom among the bathers first to cleanse themselves in the spring inside the inn and then to descend the stone stairs to the Great Spring. On three sides, the spring was fenced in by planks in the shape of a bathtub. The bottom, however, was natural rock. On the unfenced side, distorting the bathtub shape, an enormous boulder towered up like an elephant. Its glossy black surface, wet from the hot spring, was smooth and slippery. Since the story ran that you would have children if you slid down from the top of this rock into the spring, it was called the Sliding Rock.

Every time he looked up at this Sliding Rock, he thought, "This monster is mocking mankind. The people who think they have to have children, the people who think that if they slide down this rock they will have children, are all being jeered at by this gigantic, slimy face."

He permitted himself a sour smile at the black, wall-like face of the rock.

"Oh, rock, if you were to take off my old-fashioned wife's head and plunge her into the spring, I might feel a little surprised."

In the hot spring, where there were only married couples and children, his wife seemed slightly strange to him. He remembered how most of the time he forgot about her.

A woman whose hair was done in the modern ear-covering style came down the stone stairs, naked. Removing the Spanish-style hairpins, she placed them on the shelf.

"My, what a charming young lady." Saying this, she submerged herself in the spring. When she came out, the woman's freshly washed hair was like a peony with all the petals removed and only a pistil remaining.

He felt miserably shy when a woman other than a wife with her husband was in the bath, still more when it was a young woman. Forced to compare the young woman with his wife, he was swamped by self-hatred and sank into a stream of empty feelings.

"I would have cut that pine tree down and built a house myself. 'This is my wife, this is my child'—don't these words sum up all superstition? Don't they, rock?"

Beside him, his wife, flushed with the heat of the water, had closed her eyes restfully.

A wave of yellow light broke over the spring. The steam drifted up in a white fog.

"Hey there, boy! The lights have come on. How many are there?"

"Two."

"Two, huh? One on the ceiling and one on the bottom. Hey, boy, that light is strong. I'm going to dive down to the bottom. It's really strong."

The woman in the ear-covering hairdo blinked at his daughter.

"My, how clever the young lady is."

That evening, he sent his wife and child to bed ahead of him and wrote ten letters or so.

In the dressing room of the spring inside the inn, he stood rooted to the floor with astonishment. What looked like a white frog was clinging to the Sliding Rock. Facedown, she took her hands away. She kicked with her feet and slithered down the rock. The spring snickered yellowly. She crawled back up the rock and clung to it. It was that woman; her ear-covering hairdo was tightly bound up in a towel, but it was the same woman he had seen at the spring that evening.

His sash clutched in his hand, he ran up the stairs—the late-night, silent, autumnal stairs.

"That woman is coming tonight to kill my child."

His wife was asleep, her hair flowing out over the pillow, her arms around the child.

"Oh, rock, even a woman who believes in your silly superstition can frighten me this much. Perhaps my own superstition—that this is my wife, this is my child—without my knowing it is causing hundreds, maybe thousands of people to shudder with fear. Is it not so, rock?"

He felt a fresh, covetous affection toward his wife. Pulling her by the hand, he roused her.

"You—wake up!"

LD

Thank You

[1925]

This was a good year for persimmons. Autumn in the mountains was beautiful.

The harbor town was at the southern tip of the peninsula. The bus driver came down from the second floor of the terminal to the waiting area, where cheap candy shops stood in a row. He wore a purple collar on his yellow uniform. Out front stood a large red bus with a purple flag on it.

As the girl's mother stood up, gripping the neck of a paper bag of candy, she spoke to the bus driver, who was tying his shoelaces neatly.

"So it's your turn today, is it? If she has you take her there, Mr. Thank-you, she is likely to meet with good fortune. It's a sign that something good will happen."

The driver looked at the girl by the woman's side. He was silent.

"We could keep putting it off forever. . . . Besides, winter is almost upon us. It would be a shame to send this girl far away in the cold, so, if we're going to send her anyway, I thought we might as well do it while the weather's still good. I've decided to accompany her there."

The driver nodded silently; then he marched like a soldier to the bus and adjusted the cushion on the seat.

"Please sit in the front seat, ma'am. It doesn't shake as much in the front. You have a long way to go."

The woman was going to a village on the train line thirty-five miles north to sell her daughter.

As she bumped along the mountain road, the girl's eyes were fixed on the bus driver's shoulders directly ahead of her. The driver's yellow uniform filled the girl's eyes as though it were a world in itself. The mountains ahead divided and passed over each of the driver's shoulders. The bus had to cross two high mountain passes.

The bus caught up with a horse-drawn carriage. The carriage moved to the side.

"Thank you." The driver spoke in a clear voice as he bowed his head like a woodpecker, graciously, in greeting.

The bus met a horse-drawn lumber cart. The cart pulled over to the roadside.

"Thank you."

A dray.

"Thank you."

A rickshaw.

"Thank you."

A horse.

"Thank you."

Though the bus driver passed thirty vehicles in ten minutes, he never once neglected this courtesy. Even if he were to go a hundred miles, he would never relax his posture; he was like a straight cedar tree, simple and natural.

The bus left just after three o'clock. The driver had to turn on the headlights along the way. But whenever he met a horse, he turned off both headlights.

"Thank you."

"Thank you."

"Thank you."

All along the thirty-five-mile road, he was the bus driver with the best reputation among the horse-cart, pack-cart, and horse drivers.

As the bus descended into the evening darkness of the village square, the girl's body was shaking and she felt dizzy, as though her legs were floating. She clung to her mother.

"Wait a moment," the mother told her daughter and ran to the bus driver to implore him. "My daughter says she likes you. I'm asking you—I beg you with my hands clasped. Tomorrow she's going to become a plaything for a man she's never seen anyway, so . . . It's true, even a high-class girl from the city would—well, if she rode your bus just ten miles . . ."

The next morning at dawn the driver left the cheap lodging house and crossed the square like a soldier. The mother and daughter came scurrying after him. The big red bus with the purple flag pulled out of the garage and waited for the first train.

The girl got on first and stroked the black leather driver's seat as she rubbed her lips together. The mother held her sleeves together against the morning cold.

"So now I'm supposed to take her home again. This morning she cries at me, and you scold me. . . . My sympathy for her was a mistake. I *am* taking her home, all right? But only until spring. It would be a pity to send her off with the cold season coming. I can manage. But once the weather turns good, I won't be able to keep her at home."

The first train dropped off three passengers for the bus.

The driver adjusted the seat cushion. The girl's eyes were fixed on the warm shoulders directly in front of her. The autumn morning breeze flowed over both of those shoulders.

The bus caught up with a horse-drawn carriage. The carriage pulled over to the side.

"Thank you."

A pack cart.

"Thank you."

A horse.

"Thank you."

"Thank you."

"Thank you."

"Thank you."

The driver returned, full of gratitude, across the thirty-five miles of mountains and fields to the harbor town on the southern tip of the peninsula.

This was a good year for persimmons. Autumn in the mountains was beautiful.

JMH

The Silverberry Thief

[1925]

The wind is rustling
It blows in autumn

On her way home from school, a young girl was singing on the mountain road. The lacquer tree was in its fall colors. On the second floor of the weathered little inn, the windows were wide open as if unacquainted with the fall wind. The shoulders of some laborers quietly gambling upstairs could be seen from the road.

The mailman, squatting on the veranda, was trying to fit his big toe back into his torn, rubber-soled work sock. He was waiting for the woman who had received a parcel to come back out again.

"It's that kimono, is it?"

"Yes, it is."

"I thought it was about time for you to get your fall clothes."

"Now, stop that. Looking as if you knew everything there was to know about me . . ."

The woman had changed into the new lined kimono that she had taken out of the oiled-paper parcel. Seating herself on the floor of the veranda, she smoothed out the wrinkles in her lap.

"Well, that's because I read all the letters you get and all the letters you send."

"Do you think I would tell the truth in something like a letter? Not in this business."

"I'm not like you. I don't make it my business to tell lies."

"Are there any letters for me today?"

"No."

"Even letters without stamps?"

"No, I tell you."

"What are you giving me that look for? I've saved you a lot of money. When you get to be postmaster, you can make a regulation that love letters don't need stamps. But not now you can't. Writing me those smarmy love letters like stale bean jam. Then delivering them without stamps because you're the mailman. Pay the fine. I want the price of those stamps. I'm short of pocket money."

"Don't talk so loud."

"As soon as you pay up."

"I can't get out of it, I guess."

The mailman took a silver coin from his pocket and tossed it down on the porch. Then, drawing his leather pouch toward him by its strap, he stood up and stretched.

One of the laborers came thudding down the stairs in his underwear. With a sharp expression, such as God might have, a sleeping God who was tired of all His human creation, he said, "I heard a coin fall. Give it to me, sis. You borrowed fifty sen."

"I will not. It's my candy money."

Deftly retrieving the coin, the woman tucked it in her obi.

A child walked by, rolling a metal hoop that made a sound of autumn.

The daughter of the charcoal-burner was coming down the mountain with a sack of charcoal on her back. Like Momotarō returning from the subjugation of Devil Island in the fairy tale, she held a big branch of silverberries over her shoulder. The crimson berries were splendidly ripe, as if green leaves had grown on a branch of coral.

With her bag of charcoal and her bough of silverberries, she was going to the doctor's on a thank-you call.

"Is just charcoal enough?" As she had left the charcoal-burner's hut, she had asked her father, who was sick in bed.

"Tell him you had nothing else to give."

"If it were charcoal that Father had burned, it would be all right. But I'm ashamed to give charcoal that I burned. Should I wait until Father is well again and burns some?"

"Get some persimmons on the mountain."

"I'll do that, then."

But before the girl could steal the persimmons, she came to a place where there were rice paddies. The vivid red of the silverberries on the raised ridge path blew the melancholy of having to steal away from her eyes. She reached her hand to a branch. It bent without breaking. With both arms, she drew the branch down to dangle from it. Suddenly, the big branch broke off from the trunk and dropped her on her backside.

Smiling and smiling, and popping silverberries into her mouth, the girl went on down to the village. Her tongue felt rough and puckery. Some schoolgirls were on their way home.

"Give me."

"Give me."

Smiling openly, the girl silently held out the coral-like branch. The five or six children each tore off a red cluster.

The girl entered the village. The woman was on the veranda of the little inn.

"Oh, how pretty. They're silverberries, aren't they? Where are you going with them?"

"To the doctor's."

"Was it your family that came here to send a mountain palanquin for the doctor, the other day? They're prettier than red bean candy. May I have one?"

The girl held out the branch of silverberries. When the branch was resting on the woman's lap, she took her hand away from it.

"Is it all right for me to have this?"

"Yes."

"The branch and all?"

"Yes."

The woman's new silk kimono had taken the girl by surprise. Blushing, she hurried away. Looking at the branch of silverberries that spread more than twice as wide as her lap, the woman was taken by surprise. She put a berry into her mouth. Its cool sourness made her think of her own village. Not even her mother, who had sent the kimono, was there now.

A child walked by, rolling a metal hoop that made a sound of autumn.

Taking the silver coin out of her obi from behind the branch of coralline berries, the woman wrapped it in a small paper packet and quietly sat waiting for the charcoal-burner's daughter to come back on her way home.

On her way home from school, a young girl was singing on the mountain road.

The wind is rustling
It blows in autumn

LD

Summer Shoes

[1926]

Four or five old women in a horse-drawn carriage dozed off as they chatted of how this winter was a good one for oranges. The horse trotted, waving its tail as if trying to keep up with the gulls over the sea.

The driver Kanzō loved his horse. He was the only person on this road who owned a carriage for eight passengers. He was also particular about keeping his carriage the cleanest and neatest of all those on the road. As he approached a hill, he always scrambled down from the driver's seat for the horse's sake. He was secretly proud of the nimble way he could jump off and back onto the carriage. Even when he was sitting in the driver's seat, he could tell when children were hanging on to the back of the carriage by the way it rocked. He would leap down quickly and rap the children on their heads with his knuckles. So this carriage attracted the most attention among the children along the road, but it was also most frightening.

But today he had been unable to catch the children no matter how hard he had tried. He simply could not seize the flagrant offenders who dangled like monkeys from the back of his carriage. Usually, he would leap down stealthily like a cat, let the carriage pass by, and thump the children on their heads. Then he would say proudly, "Blockheads."

He jumped down again to see. This was the third time. A girl of twelve or thirteen was hurrying away, her cheeks flushed. Her eyes sparkled as her shoulders heaved with each breath. She wore a pink dress, and her socks had fallen down around her ankles. She was not wearing shoes. Kanzō glared at her. She looked away, toward the sea. Then she came trotting after the carriage.

Kanzō clicked his tongue and returned to the driver's seat. He was unaccustomed to such noble beauty as this girl's. Thinking she might have come to stay in one of the summer houses on the seashore, Kanzō had held back a bit. But he was vexed that he had not caught her, though he had jumped down three times. The girl had ridden for a mile, hanging on the back. Kanzō was so annoyed, he even used the whip on his beloved horse to make it run.

The carriage entered a small village. Kanzō blew a bugle, the horse ran faster. Looking back, he saw the girl running, her hair hanging loose on her shoulders. One of her socks dangled from her hand.

In a moment, it seemed as if she had reached the carriage. As Kanzō glanced through the glass behind the driver's seat, he got the impression that the girl was crouching in the back. But, when he jumped down for the fourth time, the girl was walking some distance behind the carriage.

"Hey, where are you going?"

The girl looked down. She was silent.

"Do you plan to hang on all the way to the harbor?"

Still she was silent.

"Are you going to the harbor?"

The girl nodded.

"Hey, your feet—look at your feet. Aren't they bleeding? You're quite a stubborn one, aren't you?"

Kanzō scowled, as was his habit. "I'll give you a ride. Get inside. It's too heavy for the horse if you hang on and ride back there, so please get inside. Come on. I don't want people to think I'm a blockhead."

He opened the carriage door for her.

Later, when he looked back from the driver's seat, he saw that the girl was sitting still, not even trying to remove the hem of her dress that had been caught in the door. Her earlier determination had vanished. Quietly, bashfully, she hung her head.

He reached the harbor a mile away, and, on the way back, the same girl suddenly appeared out of nowhere following the carriage. Kanzō obediently opened the door for her.

"Mister, I don't like riding inside. I don't want to ride inside."

"Look at the blood on your feet—the blood. Your sock is wet with blood."

Five miles down the road, the tottering carriage drew near the original village.

"Mister, let me off here, please."

As Kanzō glanced at the roadside, he saw a pair of shoes blooming white on the dry grass.

"Do you wear white shoes in winter, too?"

"But I came here in summer."

The girl put on the shoes, and, not looking back, she flew like a white heron back up the small hill to the reform school.

JMH

A Child's Viewpoint

[1926]

The young man's mother was actually dull-witted.

"My mother is trying to force me into marriage, but I have someone I've already promised."

This is how Tazuko asked for advice. And it seemed the woman was about to catch on that the promised lover was her own son. Still, the woman chattered freely, as if it were no concern of her own. "There's nothing for you to be confused about. Why, you could even leave home and marry for love. I'll warn you from my experience: I once had the same problem as you do, but I took the wrong path, and now I have been unhappy for thirty years. I think I ruined my life."

Tazuko mistakenly thought that she had an ally who approved of their love. She blushed as she spoke, "If that's true, ma'am, then do you plan to let your Ichirō marry freely?"

"Of course."

Tazuko returned home in high spirits. The young man, who had been eavesdropping, followed after her. He wrote her a letter freeing her from her promise. "Marry the one you're being pressured to." But, naturally, he could not write the following: And be sure to bear a fine child like me.

JMH

Love Suicides

[1926]

A letter came from the woman's husband. It had been two years since he had taken a dislike to his wife and deserted her. The letter came from a distant land.

"Don't let the child bounce a rubber ball. I can hear the sound. It strikes at my heart."

She took the rubber ball away from her nine-year-old daughter.

Again a letter came from her husband. It was from a different post office than the first one.

"Don't send the child to school wearing shoes. I can hear the sound. It tramples on my heart."

In place of shoes, she gave her daughter soft felt sandals. The girl cried and would no longer go to school.

Once more a letter came from her husband. It was posted only a month after the previous letter, but his handwriting suddenly looked like an old man's.

"Don't let the child eat from a porcelain bowl. I can hear the sound. It breaks my heart."

The woman fed the girl with her own chopsticks as if she were three years old. Then she remembered the time when the girl really was three years old and her husband had spent pleasant days at her side. The girl went to the cabinet on her own and took out her bowl. The woman quickly snatched it from her and dashed it against a rock in the garden: the sound of her husband's heart breaking. Suddenly the woman raised her eyebrows. She threw her own bowl against the rock. Wasn't *this* the sound of her husband's heart breaking? The woman tossed the small dinner table out into the garden. What about this sound? She threw her whole body against the wall and pounded with her fists. She flung herself at the paper partition like a spear and tumbled out on the other side. And what about this sound?

"Mommy, Mommy, Mommy!"

The girl ran toward her, crying, and the woman slapped her. Oh, listen to this sound!

Like an echo of that sound, another letter came from the woman's husband. It had been sent from yet another post office in a new distant land.

"Don't make any sound at all. Don't open or close the doors or sliding partitions. Don't breathe. The two of you mustn't even let the clocks in the house make a sound."

"The two of you, the two of you, the two of you." Tears fell as the woman whispered. Then the two of them made no sound. They ceased eternally to make even the faintest sound. In other words, the mother and daughter died.

And, strangely enough, the woman's husband lay down beside them and died, too.

JMH

The Maidens' Prayers

[1926]

"Did you see it?"

"I saw it."

"Did you see it?"

"I saw it."

The villagers gathered in the middle of the road from the mountains and fields, uneasy looks on their faces. It was uncanny enough that this many villagers should all have been looking in the same direction at the same instant, as if by prearrangement, even though they had been working scattered about the mountains and fields. And they all said they had shuddered in the same way.

The village was in a round valley, and in the center of the valley was a small hill. A stream flowed through the valley around the hill. On top of the hill was the village cemetery.

Looking from all different directions, the villagers said they had seen a gravestone tumbling down the hill like a white goblin. If it had been only one or two people who had seen it, they could have laughed it off as merely their eyes playing tricks on them, but it would have been impossible for so many people to have seen the same hallucination at the same time. I joined a group of noisy villagers, and we went up to inspect the hill.

First, we searched every inch around the foot and sides of the hill, but there was no gravestone anywhere. Then we climbed the hill and checked every grave, but all the stones were still there standing silently. Again the villagers looked at one another uneasily.

"You saw it, didn't you?"

"Yes."

"You saw it, didn't you?"

"Yes."

Repeating their questions, the villagers descended the hill, as if fleeing the cemetery. They agreed that this was certainly an omen that something bad would happen in the village. Surely it was a curse from God, or the devil, or the dead. They decided that they must pray to expel the vengeful spirit and purify the cemetery.

They gathered together the maidens of the village. Then, before the sun set, they surrounded a group of fifteen or sixteen maidens and climbed the hill. Naturally, I was among the villagers.

When the maidens were lined up in the middle of the cemetery, a gray-haired elder stood in front of them and spoke solemnly.

"Pure young girls, laugh until your bellies break. Laugh, laugh, laugh at this thing that vexes our village, and drive it away."

Then the old man laughed loudly to lead the chorus.

Simultaneously, the healthy mountain maidens all burst out laughing.

"Ha-ha. Ha-ha-ha. Ha-ha."

Overwhelmed by the volume, and drowning in this laughter that shook the valley, I added my voice as well: "Ha-ha."

One villager set fire to the dry grass in the cemetery. The maidens held their stomachs and laughed as they tossed their hair and rolled wildly on the ground; beside them, the flames lapped like the tongues of demons. When the maidens' tears of laughter dried, their eyes began to shine weirdly. If these storms of laughter could be added to the storms of nature, human beings would seem powerful enough to destroy the earth. The maidens danced madly, baring their white teeth as beasts would. What a strange and savage dance it was!

The villagers' hearts were as bright as the sun as they laughed with all their might. Suddenly I stopped laughing and knelt at one of the gravestones illuminated by the fire of the burning grass.

"God, I am pure."

But the laughter was so loud, I could not hear my own voice in my heart. The villagers laughed in harmony with the maidens until the hill was engulfed in a wave of laughter.

"Ha-ha. Ha-ha. Ha-ha. Ha-ha."

One maiden dropped a comb. It was stepped on and broken. One maiden's loosened obi was wrapped around another maiden and toppled her, and the flames spread to the end of it.

JMH

Toward Winter

[1926]

He was playing *go* with the priest of the mountain temple.

"What's happened to you? You're weak today, like a different person," the priest said.

"When the cold weather comes, I wither like a blade of grass. I'm good for nothing." He felt completely defeated, as if he could not even return the look of his opponent.

Last night, as usual, in the detached wing of the hot-spring inn, listening to the scurrying sound of the fallen leaves, he and she had talked.

"When my feet start getting cold, every year I long for home. I dream only of home."

"Since it's getting to be winter, I've begun to think that I'm unworthy of you. I'm unworthy of any woman. The thought is growing stronger."

But already their words were not reaching each other's hearts. Trying to explain, he added, "When it gets to be winter, I understand the feeling people have when they want to pray to God. It's not a humble feeling, it's a weak feeling. If I could concentrate all my thoughts on the one God and gratefully receive my daily bread, I think I would be happy. Just a bowl of rice gruel would be good."

Actually, they were having banquets every day. Only they could not leave this mountain hot spring. If all had gone as they'd wished, they probably could have rented for the summer the home that she had lost four or five years ago. But, six months earlier, without regard for the consequences, they had run away to this place and had remained here as if in hiding. The friendly people of the inn, saying nothing, had let them stay in the detached wing's single room. With no prospect of making any money, they were unable to leave. During that time, he had tired of the thing called hope. They had come to share a fatalism about everything.

"How about another game? I'll light a fire in the sunken hearth."

As he was thinking "this time," the priest unceremoniously plunked down a stone in a corner of the board right under his nose. This country priest was well pleased with himself for driving into his opponent's corner. It was galling. Suddenly losing interest, the guest felt his energy leave him.

"Didn't you have a dream last night about a defensive move? My move is Fate."

But the priest's opponent heedlessly dropped his stone onto the board. The priest gave a loud laugh.

"You fool! To have attacked the enemy with such unripe skill."

The guest's corner of the board was ignominiously invaded. Nearing the end of the campaign, the priest seized the initiative again and again. As he was disconsolately trailing him around the board, the light suddenly went out.

The priest laughed and shouted, "I'm awestruck. You've outdone the founder. Your occult power has put the founder to shame. A fool, nothing! I am awestruck. No, really, I am awestruck."

The priest got up to look for a candle. The lights going out made his opponent laugh happily for the first time all evening.

Such phrases as "Did you dream about this move last night?" and "You fool" were a habit with them whenever they played *go*. They originated in the legend of the temple's founder, a legend the priest had told him.

The temple had been built in the Tokugawa period. The founder was a samurai. His child was an imbecile. A chief retainer of his clan had ridiculed the child. Murdering the retainer, the samurai had also killed his child and fled the estate. While in hiding at this remote mountain spring, he'd had a dream. In the dream, he was sitting meditating underneath the waterfall about a mile and a half up the mountain from the hot spring. The son of the retainer appeared to avenge his father and sliced him diagonally from the left shoulder with a single stroke of his sword.

When the samurai awakened, he was in a cold sweat. What a strange dream, he thought. For one thing, he'd never thought of sitting under that waterfall. Moreover, it wasn't likely that he'd just sit there quietly gazing at the white flashing sword of his mortal enemy. It was even less likely that he, who prided himself as a swordsman even though his method differed from that taught by the clan's martial arts instructor, would be cut down by a single stroke from the likes of the chief retainer's son, even in a surprise attack. However, precisely because it was unbelievable, the dream made him uneasy. Was this his destiny? If it was fate that an imbecile child had been born to him, was it also fate that he be struck down by the sword under the waterfall? Had he not foreseen his fate in the dream? Was this not what was called a prophetic revelation? In this way, the dream had lured him to the waterfall.

"Well, then, I'll fight against my fate. I'll make it give way."

He began to visit the waterfall daily. There, sitting bolt upright on a boulder underneath torrents of water, he had waking dreams. He kept seeing a vision of a naked white blade slashing through his left shoulder. He had to escape this vision. The visionary sword must miss his shoulder and cut into the rock instead. One day, after this spiritual concentration had continued for about a month, the flashing sword of the vision grazed his shoulder and struck the rock. Jumping to his feet, he did a little dance of joy.

Of course, the same thing took place in reality as in the vision. Even when the chief retainer's son bellowed out his challenge and reviled him as a coward, the samurai sat there meditating, his eyes closed, at play on the borders of selflessness. He lost himself in the sound of the waterfall. Shutting his eyes tight, he suddenly saw the vision of the flashing sword. The chief retainer's son brought his sword down with all his might and struck the rock, benumbing his hand. The samurai opened his eyes wide.

"You fool. Do you think that by learning how to swing your sword around you can slay the gods of heaven and earth? To avoid the power of the sword, I have sought the spirits of heaven and earth. By communing with the power of heaven, I have deflected the sword of fate by just three inches."

"You fool!" After telling him this story of the founder, the priest often gleefully hurled the taunt at him, his belly shaking with laughter.

The priest came back with a candle, but the guest took his leave. Placing the candle inside a paper lantern, the priest accompanied him to the main gate of the temple. A bright, cold moon was up. There was not a single light on the mountain or in the fields.

Looking out at the mountains, the guest said, "The true joy of a moonlit night is something we no longer understand. Only the men of old, when there were no lights, could understand the true joy of a moonlit night."

"That's so." The priest, also, looked out at the mountains.

"Lately, when I've gone up the mountain, the deer have been calling to each other. It's the mating season."

"And my own mate?" He asked himself this as he made his way down the stone stairs of the temple. "She's probably lying on top of the quilt, as usual, with her head on her elbow."

The past few evenings, the maid had laid out the bedding early. But he didn't go to bed. It was too much trouble to burrow under the covers. Stretching himself out on top of the quilt, he would draw his feet up inside the skirt of his padded kimono and rest his head on his elbow. At some point, his habit had transferred itself to her. And so, each night, from evening on, vaguely sprawled out on the two sets of bedding in the same way, they lay there, their eyes turned away from each other.

Her figure, as he went out through the temple gate, floated up like a vision of his fate. Was he to be the only one who could not make fate give way?

"Get up off that bed and sit up straight," he ordered her in his heart.

"Ah!" The lantern was shaking wildly in his hand.

He felt the coldness of the night, getting on toward winter, against his eyelids.

LD

The Sparrow's Matchmaking

[1926]

Long accustomed to a life of self-indulgent solitude, he began to yearn for the beauty of giving himself to others. The nobility of the word *sacrifice* became clear to him. He took satisfaction in the feeling of his own littleness as a single seed whose purpose was to carry forward from the past to the future the life of the species called humanity. He even sympathized with the thought that the human species, together with the various kinds of minerals and plants, was no more than a small pillar that helped support a single vast organism adrift in the cosmos—and with the thought that it was no more precious than the other animals and plants.

"All right."

His elder cousin spun a silver coin on the mirror stand. Then, slapping it flat under her palm, she looked at him with a serious face. He rested his languid, melancholy gaze on her white hand. Then he said brightly, "Tails."

"Tails? But you've got to decide beforehand. If it comes out tails, will you marry that person or not?"

"Let's say I will."

"Ah, it's heads."

"Is that so?"

"What kind of foolish answer is that?"

His cousin gave a loud laugh. Throwing down the photograph of the girl, she got up and left the room. She was a woman who laughed a lot. Her clear, laughing voice went on for a long time. In all the men of the house, it caused a strange kind of aural jealousy.

Picking up the photograph, he looked at the girl. It would be good to marry this girl, he thought. If he could feel this degree of affection, there must still be many girls in Japan who would marry him, entrusting their fate to their elder brothers and fathers. That was beautiful, he thought. What was ugly was himself, lost because he'd awakened to a trivial self-awareness.

"When you come right down to it, choosing a marriage partner is really like a lottery. It's like deciding by tossing a coin." When his cousin had said this, he'd even felt exhilarated at the idea of entrusting his fate to the silver coin underneath her white palm. But, when he realized that she was merely teasing him, he turned his lonely look to the miniature lake at the edge of the veranda.

If there is another girl who ought to be my wife, show me her face reflected in the water, he prayed to the lake. He believed that it was possible to see right through time and space. That was how lonely he was.

As he looked intently at the water's surface, a black, pointy stone thrown by God plummeted into his field of vision. A pair of mating sparrows had fallen from the roof. Flapping their wings in the water, the two came apart and flew up in different directions. He understood this flashing glimpse of God.

"Is that how it is," he muttered.

The ripples on the water's surface spread out and grew calm again. He went on looking intently at the lake. His heart became a mirror like the calm surface of the water. Suddenly, a single sparrow was clearly reflected there. The sparrow was singing. The meaning of the song was this:

"You who are lost probably would not believe me even if I were to show you the image of the woman who is to be your wife in this world. And so I will show you the image of your wife in the next world."

He spoke to the sparrow, "Sparrow, I thank you. If I am to be reborn as a sparrow and marry you in the next world, then I will marry this girl. A person who has seen his fate in the world to come will not be lost in this world. My lovely, precious wife of the next world has made a marriage for me in this one."

And then, with a clear-hearted greeting to the girl in the photograph, he felt the greatness of God.

LD

The Hat Incident

[1926]

It was summer. Every morning the lotuses in Ueno's Shinobazu Pond opened their flowers with a lovely bursting sound.

The incident described here occurred in the evening on the moon-viewing bridge that crosses the pond.

The people who had come to enjoy the cool of the evening decorated the bridge railing like rosary beads. The breeze blew from the south. Even when the nimble shop curtain of the ice-house hung down motionless in the town, a delicate breeze would be blowing here that made the reflection of the moon look like a fish with golden scales. Still, the breeze was not enough to turn the leaves of the lotuses.

The regular visitors who came to seek the evening cool knew the path the breeze took. They promptly crossed the bridge, stepped over the metal railing, and stood on the edge. Taking off their clogs, they placed them side by side and sat on them. Then they took off their hats and put them on their knees or beside them.

Advertising lights spilled onto the south end of the pond:

HOTAN

BLUTOSE

UTSU BRAND TONIC

LION TOOTHPASTE

Some of the visitors, who appeared to be workmen, began to talk.

"Hotan has the largest neon letters. It's quite an old, established company."

"That's the main store over there, isn't it?"

"Recently, even Hotan has lost business, hasn't it?"

"But, for that kind of medicine, Hotan is definitely the best."

"Is it?"

"Of course. Jintan only sells because they advertise so much."

"Damn!" a young man two or three places over exclaimed as he grasped the edge of the bridge and looked down. A straw hat was floating on the pond.

The visitors around him all chuckled. The man who had dropped the hat blushed and started to leave.

"Hey, you. You!" said a stern voice. The man who had called out caught the sleeve of the man who had dropped the hat. "Why don't you pick it up? It'll be easy."

The man who had dropped the hat was taken aback. He looked around at this thin man and immediately forced a weak smile. "It's all right. I can buy a new one. It's probably better after all."

"Why is that?" the thin man asked in a strangely sharp tone.

"What do you mean 'why'? It's an old hat from last year, so it's about time I bought a new one. And, besides, it's all wet. Straw gets waterlogged."

"So wouldn't it be better to pick it up before it gets waterlogged?"

"I couldn't reach it if I tried. It's all right."

"You can reach it. If you put both hands on the edge like this and hang from the bridge, you can reach it with your feet." The thin man stuck his rear out over the pond as if he would show the man how to do it. "I'll hold one of your hands from above."

The people laughed at the thin man's pose. Three or four got up and moved closer. They spoke to the man who had dropped his hat.

"Well, you should pick it up. It doesn't do much good to have a pond wearing a hat."

"That's right. Such a little hat for such a big pond. Casting pearls before swine—and hats before ponds. You ought to pick it up."

The man who dropped the hat began to show his hostility at the gathering crowd. "It wouldn't do any good to try to pick it up."

"Go ahead and try. If the hat isn't any good, you can give it to some beggar."

"I wish I'd dropped it on some beggar's head to begin with."

The thin man was very serious amid the crowd's laughter. "If you keep dawdling, it's going to float away."

Then the thin man held the railing post with one hand and stretched the other toward the water. "Hold on to this hand—"

"I'm supposed to pick that up?" The man who had dropped the hat spoke as if it were not his own.

"Yes, you are."

"Well"—the man who had dropped the hat took off his clogs and got ready—"hold on to my hand tightly."

This so surprised the sightseers that the laughter stopped all at once.

Grasping the thin man's hand with his right hand and putting his left hand on the edge of the bridge, the man slid his legs down the bridge pylon. Then he dangled his feet until they reached the water. He caught the top of the floating hat with his feet. Then he grabbed the brim of the hat with the toes of one foot. Raising his right shoulder, he put his left elbow on the edge of the bridge. He pulled hard with his right hand.

At that moment, he splashed into the pond. The thin man, who had been holding his right hand, had suddenly let go.

"Oh!"

"He fell!"

"He fell!"

The onlookers were all clamoring for a better view when they were suddenly pushed from behind and plunged into the pond, too. The thin man's clear, high laughter could be heard above the uproar.

The thin man scampered across the bridge like a black dog and ran off into the dark town.

"He ran away!"

"Damn it!"

"Was he a pickpocket?"

"A madman?"

"A detective?"

"He's the *tengu** of Ueno Mountain!"

"He's the *kappa* of Shinobazu Pond!"

JMH

*Trans. note: *Tengu* are goblins common in Japanese folklore. *Kappa* are water creatures that often play tricks on human beings in Japanese folktales.

One Person's Happiness

[1926]

"Dear Elder Sister,

"I haven't written in a long time. I hope you are in good health. Kii, too, must be very cold by this time of year. Here, every day, it goes down to more than twenty degrees below zero. The windows of the house are all frosted. I'm healthy, but cracks have opened up on my hands and I have cold sores on my feet. Even walking is hard. That's to be expected. Every morning I get up at five and cook the rice, heat the water, and make bean paste soup. Breakfast is at six. When breakfast is over, I clean up, but it's always with freezing-cold water. School starts at nine, but every day until eight-thirty I do housework. The hardest job is cleaning the house inside and out and the privy. For this, too, I have to use water.

"School is over at either two-thirty or three. But if I'm not back by three when it ends at two-thirty, or three-thirty when it ends at three, I'm scolded at supper. When I get home, first I have to do housework and then chop up kindling for the next day's bathwater. Sometimes the snow is blowing all around and I can't see an inch in front of me. My hands are numb, and my feet are so cold they ache. And the cold snow blows down inside my collar. When I see the fresh, warm blood oozing out of the sores on my feet, tears come to my eyes. When I'm through, I have to start getting supper ready. Supper is over by five. After I've cleaned up, I have to take care of Saburō until he falls asleep. I don't have a minute left over for homework.

"Then, on Sundays, I have to wash my shirts and pants and things, and sometimes my father's socks and gloves, all in cold water. If there's any time, I have to look after Saburō. Day after day I work like this. The money I need for school supplies I finally get after being scolded twenty times, but there are all sorts of things I'm short of, so that I'm scolded by the teachers, too. Lately my grades have gone way down, and I have the feeling my health is weaker as well.

"This New Year's, too, I did nothing but housework all day every day. My parents ate a lot of their favorite things, but during the three days of New Year's all they gave me was a single tangerine. I don't have to tell you how it is the rest of the time. Something happened on the second day of New Year's. Just because I burned the rice, I was hit on the head so hard it would have bent a pair of fire tongs. Even now, my head sometimes aches terribly.

"When I think back about how I was taken away when I was six from Grandfather and Grandmother before I knew what was happening by my devil of a father and brought to this cold Manchuria where I've spent ten years of hardship, I wonder why I was born to be such an unfortunate child. Every day, I am beaten with a stick the way you would beat an animal. I'm beaten with a long-stemmed pipe, though I don't think I do anything that bad.

"Everything you hear from my mother is just lies that she makes up. But, a month from now, I'll be graduating. I'm going to leave this awful house behind me and go to Osaka. I'll work as an office boy during the day and study as hard as I can at night school.

"Please be healthy and strong, Kachiko. Please give my love to Grandfather and Grandmother in Kumano. Good-bye."

While he was reading this letter, which he had snatched away from Kachiko, she sat absolutely still.

"Do they make even a boy do this kind of work?"

"I thought to make even a man do this kind of work . . ."

". . . to make even a man do this kind of work," he said after her. He put all his sympathy into the words. "Was your life like this when you were in Manchuria?"

"It was worse."

For the first time, he understood Kachiko's feelings when, as a girl of thirteen, she had come all by herself from Manchuria to Kii. Until now, he had only felt surprise at the girl's bravery.

"What do you mean to do?"

"I'm going to put my brother in school. Whatever happens, I'm going to put him in school."

"Then you should send him travel money and tell him to come right away."

"Now is bad. Even if he could get on a train, he'd be caught at one of the stations along the way. Or he'd be sure to be caught when he rode the ferry. My father plans to sell my brother when he graduates this spring from upper grade school. I was threatened with that every day myself. 'I'm going to sell you, I'm going to sell you.' I thought I might send money to the place my brother was sold to and buy him back."

"That's no good either. If it's somewhere in Manchuria, how will you find out where he's been sold to and what he's doing?"

"It can't be helped. If he's caught along the way and taken back, he might even be killed."

Kachiko looked at the floor.

Kachiko, for a year now, had nursed him through his illness. He had begun to feel that he could not part with Kachiko. The world said that if he, a married man, loved Kachiko more than he already did, it would lead her into misfortune, but he had made up his mind. Even if it meant misfortune, it could not be helped. At that point, her younger brother's letter had come. The letter made his cheeks turn cold. How could he dare bring further misfortune on this girl, who had fled for her life to a faraway place from a childhood even harsher than her brother's? There his feelings had halted. However, he was convalescing now.

He made his decision. He would go to Manchuria and take the boy away from the stepmother. And he would send him to school.

He was happy. If he helped her brother, his life could remain in contact with Kachiko's. And it was clearly within his power to bring happiness to the boy. If, just once during his lifetime, he could make one other person happy, then he, too, would be happy.

LD

There Is a God

[1926]

As evening drew on, a single star, shining like a gaslight on the shoulder of the mountain, startled him. He had never seen a star this big and this near. Pierced by its light, feeling the cold, he came back down the white-pebbled road like a fox on the run. It was so still that not a single fallen leaf stirred.

Dashing into the bathhouse, he leapt into the hot spring. Only when he put the hot wet cloth to his face did the cold star fall from his cheek.

"It's gotten cold. Will you be here for New Year's as well?"

When he looked around, he saw that the speaker was the poultryman, whom he recognized from the inn.

"No, I'm thinking of crossing the mountains to the south."

"The south is beautiful. We were in Yama-minami until three or four years ago. When it gets to be winter, I always want to go south." As he spoke, the poultryman did not try to look at him. So he took a stealthy look at the poultryman's strange actions. Kneeling in the bath and reaching up, he was washing the breasts of his wife, who sat on the edge of the tub.

The young wife, pushing out her breasts as though to give them to her husband, kept her eyes fastened on her husband's head. On her narrow chest, the small breasts swelled meagerly like white sake cups. They were a sign of her childish purity. Because of ill health, she would always have the body of a girl. This body, like the soft stem of a plant, made the beautiful face it supported all the more flowerlike.

"Will it be the first time you've been south of the mountains?"

"No. I was there five or six years ago."

"Oh, is that so?"

Holding his wife around the shoulder with one hand, the poultryman rinsed off the frothy soap from her chest.

"There was an old man with palsy in the teahouse at the pass. I wonder if he's still there."

I've said a bad thing, he thought. The poultryman's wife also seemed to be crippled in her arms and legs.

"An old man in the teahouse? Who could that be, I wonder?"

The poultryman turned toward him. The wife said casually, "That old man? He died three or four years ago."

"Oh, is that so?" For the first time, he looked squarely at the wife's face. Then, instantly averting his eyes, he covered his face with the washcloth.

It's that girl, he thought.

He wanted to hide himself in the evening clouds of steam rising from the bath. He felt ashamed of his nakedness. She was the girl he had seduced in Yama-minami during his trip there five or six years ago. Because of her, his conscience had hurt him ever since. But he had continued to have a distant dream of her. Even so, to meet her in the bath of this inn was an excessively cruel coincidence. Suffocating, he took the washcloth away from his face.

The poultryman, no longer talking with a virtual stranger like himself, stepped out of the bath and went around behind his wife.

"Here, go into the water just once."

The wife opened her slender, pointed elbows slightly. Holding her under the arms, the poultryman lightly lifted her. Like an intelligent cat, she drew in her arms and legs. The ripples she made as she entered the water lapped gently at the other man's chin. The poultryman, jumping in after her, began busily splashing water over his balding head.

Covertly observing her, the other man saw that she had frowned and closed her eyes tightly, perhaps because of the hot steam permeating her body. The abundant hair that had surprised him even in her girlhood tumbled awry, losing its shape like a weighty ornament.

The tub was large enough to swim around in. She did not seem to have noticed that it was he who sat submerged in one corner. As if praying to her, he sought her forgiveness. Her having been crippled by illness might also be due to his sin. Her body, like a white sorrow, was telling him to his face that she had suffered this way because of him.

The poultryman's extraordinary gentleness toward his young, crippled wife had become the talk of the hot-spring inn. Everybody regarded the act of this forty-year-old man carrying his wife on his back into the bath every day as a poem inspired by her frail health. Most of the time, though, the man took her to the village bathhouse and did not come to the one at the inn. So it was not surprising that he had not known that the poultryman's wife was that girl.

As if the poultryman had forgotten that the other man was there, he left the tub ahead of his wife and spread out her clothing on the steps of the bath. When he'd put it all together, from undergarments to Japanese coat, he lifted his wife out of the water. Held from behind, again like an intelligent cat, she drew in her arms and legs. Her round kneecaps glistened like opals. Making her sit down on her clothes, raising her chin with one middle finger, the husband wiped her throat dry and combed up her stray hairs. Then, as if enfolding the naked pistils in the petals, he wrapped her up in her clothes.

When he'd tied her sash, he gently lifted her onto his back

and set off toward the inn along the dry riverbed. The empty bed was full of a faint moonlight. Her legs, trembling whitely underneath, were smaller than her husband's arms, which held her in a clumsy half-encirclement.

As he watched the poultryman's retreating figure, tears gently fell from his eyes to the surface of the bath. Involuntarily, with a feeling of humility, he murmured, "There is a God."

He understood that his having thought he had made her unhappy was a mistake. He understood that he had failed to know his proper place. He understood that human beings cannot make other human beings unhappy. He understood also that it was a mistake to have sought her forgiveness. He understood that it was conceit for a person who has raised himself by wronging another to seek forgiveness from the person laid low by the wrong. He understood that human beings cannot wrong other human beings.

"God, I have lost to you."

Feeling as if he were being carried along on that murmuring voice, he listened to the sound of the softly flowing mountain stream.

LD

Goldfish on the Roof

[1926]

There was a large mirror at the head of Chiyoko's bed.

Every night, when she let her hair down and buried one cheek in the pillow, she would gaze quietly at the mirror. A vision of thirty or forty lionhead goldfish would appear there, like red artificial flowers submerged in a water tank. Some nights the moon was also reflected among them.

But the moon did not shine on the mirror through the window; instead, Chiyoko would see the reflection of the moon as it fell on the water in the tanks of the rooftop garden. The mirror was a silver curtain of illusion. Her mind was worn down like a phonograph needle because of the clarity of these visions. Feeling unable to leave her bed, there she grew dismally older. Only her black hair, which lay disheveled on her white pillow, would always retain a youthful richness.

One night, a lacewing was crawling lightly on the mahogany frame of the mirror. Chiyoko jumped out of bed and pounded on her father's bedroom door.

"Father, Father, Father!"

Tugging at her father's sleeve, her knuckles white, she dashed up to the rooftop garden.

One of the lionhead goldfish was dead, floating with its belly upward as if pregnant with some strange creature.

"Father, I'm sorry. Will you forgive me? Won't you forgive me? I don't sleep. I keep watch over them at night, too . . ."

Her father did not speak. He merely gazed around at the six tanks as though he were looking at men's coffins.

It was after her father came from Peking that he built tanks on the rooftop and began to raise fish.

He had lived with a concubine in Peking for a long time. Chiyoko was the daughter of that concubine.

Chiyoko was sixteen when they returned to Japan. It was winter. Tables and chairs from Peking were scattered about the antique Japanese room. Her older half-sister was sitting in a chair. Chiyoko was sitting on the mat floor, looking up at her.

"I'll soon become a member of another family, so it's all right. But you are not Father's real child. You came to this house and my mother took care of you. Just don't forget that."

When Chiyoko looked down, her older sister put both her feet on Chiyoko's shoulders, then lifted Chiyoko's chin with one foot to make her look up. Chiyoko held her sister's feet and cried. As she held them, her sister worked both feet into the bosom of Chiyoko's kimono.

"Oh, it's so warm. Take off my socks and warm my feet."

Crying, Chiyoko removed her sister's socks and held her feet against her breast.

Soon, the Japanese-style house was remodeled in a Western style. The father placed the six goldfish tanks on the rooftop and was there from morning until night. He invited goldfish specialists from all over the country to his house, and he took the fish to expositions, two or even four hundred miles away.

Eventually, Chiyoko began to care for the fish. Growing more and more melancholy day by day, she did nothing but gaze at them.

Chiyoko's real mother had returned to Japan and taken up separate lodging, but soon she became hysterical. After she calmed down, she grew gloomy and silent. The beauty of Chiyoko's mother's face had not changed in the least since she was in Peking, but her complexion suddenly turned strangely dark.

There were many young suitors among those who came and went in her father's house. She said to the young men, "Please bring me some fish food, some water fleas. I'm going to feed some to the fish."

"Where can I find them?"

"You might look around in a ditch."

But every night she stared into the mirror. She grew gloomily older. She turned twenty-six.

Her father died. When they opened the seal on his will, it said, "Chiyoko is not my child."

She ran to her bedroom to cry. When she glanced at the mirror at the head of her bed, she screamed and dashed up to the rooftop garden.

Where had she come from? And when? Her mother was standing by the fish tank, her face dark. Her mouth was full of lionhead fish. The tail of one of them dangled from her mouth like a tongue. Though the woman saw her daughter, she ignored her as she ate the fish.

"Oh, Father!" The girl screamed and struck her mother. Her mother tumbled against the glazed brick and died with the goldfish in her mouth.

With this, Chiyoko was freed from her mother and father. She regained her youth and set out on a life of happiness.

JMH

Mother

[1926]

1 / The Husband's Diary

Tonight I took a wife
When I embraced her—the womanly softness
My mother was also a woman
Tears overflowing, I told my new bride
Become a good mother
Become a good mother
For I never knew my mother

2 / The Husband's Illness

It was warm enough for the swallows to have come. The petals of the magnolia tree in the garden of the house next door looked like white boats as they fell. Inside the glass door, the wife wiped her husband's body with alcohol. He was so thin that grime collected in the hollows between his ribs.

"You look as though . . . Well, you and your illness want to commit a love suicide together."

"Maybe so. Since it's a lung disease, the bug is eating toward my heart."

"That's right. Those germs are closer to your heart than I am. When you fell ill, the first thing you did was to become terribly selfish. You've spitefully closed the door through which I used to reach inside you. If you could walk, you would surely leave and abandon me."

"That's because I don't want to commit a three-way love suicide—me, you, and the bug."

"A three-way suicide would be fine. I don't want to just casually look on as the two of you commit suicide. Even if your mother did catch your father's disease, *I* won't catch your disease. What happened to the parents does not necessarily happen to the child."

"That's true. I didn't know if I would come down with the same illness my parents had until I got sick. But I *have* come down with the same disease."

"That's all right, isn't it? Perhaps I had better catch it. Then you wouldn't try to stay away from me."

"Think about our child."

"Our child—what do you mean?"

"You don't understand how I feel. You don't understand; your mother is alive."

"That's a prejudice—a prejudice. When you talk to me like that, I get so vexed I want to kill my mother. I want to swallow some germs. And I will, I will!"

Screaming, she flew toward her husband, aiming for his lips. He grabbed her collar.

"Give me the germs. Give them to me." His wife writhed. He forced her to the floor with just the strength in his bones. He lay on top of her. Her kimono was open. He spat blood on her white round breast and rolled to the floor.

"D-D-Don't give this breast to the child."

3 / The Wife's Illness

"Mother, Mother, Mother!"

"I'm here. I'm alive."

"Mother!"

The child was still bumping against the sliding partition of the sickroom.

"You mustn't let him in. You mustn't."

"You're mean."

The wife closed her eyes as if giving up. She dropped her head back onto the pillow.

"I was just like that boy. I wasn't allowed in my mother's sickroom. I cried outside," her husband said.

"It's the same fate," said the wife.

"Fate? Even if I die, I don't want you to use the word 'fate.' I hate it."

The child was crying in some corner of the house. The nightwatchman passed by, sounding a wooden clapper. He could be heard breaking icicles from the water pipes with a metal rod.

"You don't remember your mother, do you?" the wife asked.

"No, I don't."

"You were three years old when she died, weren't you?"

"Yes, three."

"That child is also three."

"But, as I grow older, I think that the time will come when I suddenly recall my mother's face."

"If you had seen your mother's dead face, I think surely you would have remembered it."

"No, I only remember banging myself against the partition. If I had been able to see her as much as I pleased, quite the contrary, I'm certain I wouldn't have remembered anything about my mother."

His wife closed her eyes for a moment. Then she spoke. "We are unfortunate to have been born in an age of unbelief—an age that does not think of life after death."

"And now is the most unhappy time for the dead. But, an

age when the dead will be happy, an age of wisdom, will surely come soon."

"Perhaps so."

The wife recalled all the times she and her husband had traveled far together. Then she continued to have all kinds of beautiful hallucinations. She took her husband's hand as if awakening. "I . . . ," she said quietly. "I think I am fortunate to have married you. You believe me, don't you, that I don't at all resent having caught your illness?"

"I believe you."

"So, when that child grows up, be sure he gets married."

"I understand."

"You suffered a lot before we were married, didn't you? You thought you'd get the same illness your parents had, that your wife would also become infected, and that you'd have a child who would become ill, too. But our marriage has made me happy. I think that is enough for me. So don't let him taste unnecessary sadness and suffer, thinking it would be bad to marry. Permit him the joy of marriage. This is my last wish."

4 / The Husband's Diary

Tonight I took a wife
When I embraced her—the womanly softness
My mother was also a woman
Tears overflowing, I told my new bride
Become a good mother
Become a good mother
For I never knew my mother

JMH

Morning Nails

[1926]

A poor girl lived in a rented room on the second floor of a shabby house. She was waiting to marry her fiancé, but every night a different man came to her room. The morning sun did not shine on this house. The girl often did laundry outside the back door, wearing men's worn-out clogs.

Every night the men would say the same thing. "What's this? Don't you have a mosquito net?"

"I'm sorry. I'll stay awake all night and keep the mosquitoes off. Please forgive me."

The girl would nervously light a green mosquito coil, then turn off the lamp. As she gazed at the tiny glow, she would recall her childhood. She always fanned the men's bodies. She dreamed of waving a fan.

It was already early autumn.

An old man came to the second-floor room—an unusual occurrence.

"Aren't you going to put up a mosquito net?"

"I'm sorry. I'll stay awake all night and keep the mosquitoes off. Please forgive me."

"Oh, wait a moment," the old man said as he stood up.

The girl tugged at him. "I'll keep the mosquitoes off until morning. I won't sleep at all."

"I'll be right back."

The old man descended the stairs. With the lamp on, the girl lit the coil. Alone in the brightly lighted room, she found it impossible to recall her childhood days.

The old man returned in about an hour. The girl jumped up.

"I'm glad you at least have hooks for the net already in the ceiling."

The old man hung the new white mosquito net in the shabby room. The girl went inside it. As she spread out the skirt of the net, her heart beat faster at its refreshing feel.

"I knew you would come back, so I waited without turning off the lamp. I want to look at this new white net a little longer in the light."

But the girl fell into a deep sleep that she had awaited for months. She did not even know when the old man left in the morning.

"Hey . . . hey . . ."

She awoke to the sound of her fiancé's voice.

"After all this time, we can finally get married tomorrow! . . . That's a nice mosquito net. It makes me feel refreshed just to look at it." He unhooked the net as he spoke and pulled the girl from beneath it. He placed her on top. "Sit right here on the net. It looks like a giant white lotus. It makes the room look pure . . . like you."

The touch of the new linen made her feel like a new bride.

"I'm going to cut my toenails." Sitting on the white net that filled the room, the girl began innocently to cut her long-neglected nails.

JMH

The Young Lady of Suruga

[1927]

"Oh, how I wish we lived around Gotenba. It's an hour and a half."

The train had arrived at Gotenba Station. Raising both her knees like a grasshopper, the girl stamped on the floor of the passenger car. Her face glued to the window, she watched as her classmates childishly nodded farewell from the platform. She spoke as if she would like to shrug her shoulders in boredom.

At Gotenba, it suddenly gets lonely on the train. Those who have made a long trip on the local rather than the express train will know this. At seven or eight in the morning and at two or three in the afternoon, the train fills up with a bouquet of flowers. How bright and noisy it becomes with the crowd of girls that go to and from school on these trains! And how short that lively time is. At the next stop, only ten minutes away, fifty girls have become none at all. Yet on my train trips, I have had such diverse impressions of so many girls from different places.

However, this time I was not on a long trip. I was going from Izu to Tokyo. At that time I was living in the mountains of Izu. From Izu, you change at Mishima for the Tokkaidō Line. On my train there was always this time of flowers. The girls were students from the girls' schools of Mishima and Numazu. I went up to Tokyo once or twice a month, and in the course of a year and a half I had gotten to know about twenty girls by sight. I remembered the feelings of the time when I had gone to middle school on the train. I ended by learning what car of the train those girls generally would be in.

This time also I was in the second car from the back. When the girl had said, "It's an hour and a half," she had meant from Numazu to Suruga. She was a young lady of Suruga. If you're a person who has gone beyond Hakone on the train, you probably know it. Suruga is a town where the girl workers in the big spinning mill across the mountain river wave white kerchiefs at the train from the factory windows and grounds. This girl was probably the daughter of an engineer or technician employed by the silk company. She usually rode in the second car from the back. She was the most beautiful and high-spirited of them all.

It was an hour and a half on the train, coming and going, twice a day. It must have been so long for her that her young doe's body grew stale and restless. Furthermore it was winter, so that she had to leave the house while it was still dark, and return after it had gotten dark. The train arrived at Suruga at 5:18. But for me, that hour and a half was all too short. It was too short to watch vaguely without looking at her as she chattered away, took a schoolbook out of her bag, did knitting, or teased her friends in the other seats. When we got to Gotenba, there was not much more than twenty minutes left.

Like her, I watched the schoolgirls walking on the rainy platform until they were out of sight. It being December, the station lights were already gleaming moistly in the dusk. On the distant dark mountains, the flames of a forest fire floated up vividly.

With a solemnity totally unlike her liveliness until then, the girl started to talk in whispers to a friend. She was graduating next March. She was entering a women's college in Tokyo. That was evidently what they were talking about.

We came to Suruga. From now on there would not be one

schoolgirl on the train. The rain drove against the window my face was pressed against as I watched her go.

"Oh, miss!" Wasn't there another girl who had run up to her when she got off, and hugged her hard?

"Oh!"

"I waited for you. I could have gone up on the two o'clock train. But I wanted to see you before I went . . ."

Under an umbrella, forgetting the rain, their cheeks almost touching, the two girls chatted busily. The train whistle blew. Hurriedly boarding the train, the other girl stuck her head out a window.

"When I go to Tokyo, we can see each other. Please come to my school dormitory."

"I can't come."

"Oh! Why can't you?"

The two put on separate, sad faces. The second girl must have been a worker at the spinning mill. She was leaving the company and going to Tokyo, but had waited nearly three hours to meet this schoolgirl.

"Let's meet in the city, then."

"Yes."

"Good-bye."

"Good-bye."

The factory girl's shoulders were soaking wet from the rain. Probably the schoolgirl's were, too.

LD

Yuriko

[1927]

When she was in grade school, Yuriko thought to herself, "I feel so sorry for Umeko*—having to use a pencil smaller than her thumb and carrying around her big brother's old book satchel."

So that she would have the same things as her best-loved friend, she cut her long pencil into several smaller ones with the little saw attached to her penknife. Since she did not have a big brother, she tearfully begged her parents to buy her a boy's briefcase.

When she was in girls' school, Yuriko thought to herself, "Matsuko is so beautiful. When her earlobes and fingers get all red and chapped with frostbite, she's adorable."

So that she would be the same as her best-loved friend, she soaked her hands for a long time in the cold water of the wash-basin. Moistening her ears, she set out for school in the cold morning wind.

When she graduated from girls' school and got married, it goes without saying that Yuriko loved her husband to distraction. So, emulating the best-loved person in her life, she cut her hair, wore thick spectacles, cultivated the down on her upper lip in the hope that it would become a mustache, smoked a seaman's

*Trans. note: All the girls' names in this story are the names of flowers and trees: Umeko (plum child), Matsuko (pine child), and Yuriko (lily child).

pipe, said "Hey" to her husband, walked with a bouncy man's step, and tried to sign up for the army. Astonishingly enough, her husband forbade her each and every one of these things. He even complained about her wearing the same long underwear as himself. He grimaced when, like himself, she didn't put on any rouge or powder. And so her love for him was bound hand and foot. Like a plant whose buds have been snipped off, it went on slowly withering.

"What an unpleasant person," she thought. "Why doesn't he let me do the same as him? It's just too lonely when the person I love and I are different."

And so Yuriko fell in love with God. She prayed, "God, please show yourself to me. Somehow show yourself. I want to become the same as the God I love and do the same things."

The voice of God, fresh and clear, came echoing down from the sky.

"You shall become a lily, like the *yuri* in your name. Like the lily, you shall not love anything. Like the lily, you shall love everything."

"Yes."

Answering meekly, Yuriko turned into a lily.

LD

God's Bones

[1927]

Mr. Kasahara Seiichi, managing director of a suburban trolley-car company; Takamura Tokijurō, actor in historical movies; Tsujii Morio, medical student at a private university; and Mr. Sakuma Benji, owner of the Canton Restaurant—each had received the same letter from Yumiko, a waitress at the Blue Heron coffee shop.

"I am sending you the bones. They are the bones of God. My baby lived a day and a half. It had no strength from the moment it was born. I just looked on as the nurse held it upside down by the feet and shook it. It finally burst out crying. Yesterday, at noon, I'm told, it gave two yawns and died. And yet the baby in the bed next to mine—of course, it was born in the seventh month—as soon as it was born, it let out a stream of piss and died on the spot.

"The baby didn't resemble anyone. It didn't even resemble me the least little bit. It was just like a beautiful little doll. Please imagine a baby with the most adorable face in the world. It had no identifying marks or any defects. It had plump cheeks, and its lips were closed, with a little thin blood on them after it died. Other than that, I can't remember anything. The nurses praised it, saying it was such a lovable child, with such fair skin.

"If it was meant to be an unfortunate child, if it would have been weak even had it lived, I think it is better that it died before it drank my milk or laughed. I wept for this child who was born not resembling anyone. Didn't this baby, in its baby's heart, while it was still in the womb, say to itself, I can't resemble anyone? It came into this world with that kind of pathetic thoughtfulness. And didn't it leave this world thinking, I have to die before I start to resemble anyone?

"You—no, it's better to say clearly, all of you—all of you, up to now, even if I'd slept with a hundred men, a thousand men, would have put on know-nothing faces, as if that sort of thing were of no more account than the number of wooden paving-blocks in the street. Yet when I got pregnant, my, what a fuss you all made. All of you gentlemen—it was just like you to do it—came with a big masculine microscope to peer at a woman's secrets.

"Hakuin, the priest—it's a story from the old days, but he took the baby of an unmarried girl in his arms and said, 'This is my child.' God has rescued my child, too. To the baby in the womb, when it was sadly thinking about whom it should resemble, God said, 'My dearly beloved child, resemble me. Be born as a god. Because you are God's child.'

"Because of the heartbreaking thoughtfulness of this child, I cannot say which of you I wanted the child to resemble. And so I am sending all of you a share of the ashes."

The managing director, who'd hurriedly jammed the small white paper box into his pocket, furtively opened it inside the car. Back at the office, summoning the beautiful typist for dictation, he decided to have a smoke. When he reached into his pocket, the box of ashes came out with the pack of Happy Hits.

The restaurant owner, sniffing at the ashes, opened his safe and placed the box inside, taking out yesterday's receipts to send them to the bank.

The medical student was riding on the Government Railway Line when the box of ashes in his pocket was crushed by the hard, lilac-white thigh of a schoolgirl, thrown against him by a lurch of the trolley. He said to himself, "I think I'll marry this girl." He was stirred up by a lively lust.

The movie actor, slipping the ashes into a secret pouch in which he kept fish skins and Spanish fly, rushed off for a shooting session.

A month later, Kasahara Seiichi came to the Blue Heron and said to Yumiko, "You should bury those ashes at a temple. Why are you holding on to them?"

"Who, me? I gave all of the ashes to all of you. Why should I have any?"

LD

A Smile Outside the Night Stall

[1927]

I stopped short. It must have been two hours since the Hakuhin, a building that always closes at the same time in the evening, had tightly shut its doors. My back to those doors on the thoroughfare in Ueno, I had stopped in front of a firecracker stand and an optician's stall. I had been looking at the crowds on the pavement from evening into night, and, to my eyes, the dirt sidewalk, whose breadth was the space between the Hakuhin and the night stalls, seemed curiously wide, so that I felt shy about walking down the middle of it. Each time a belated pedestrian went by, the color of the packed, water-sprinkled dirt sank all the more blackly into itself, and the scraps of wastepaper floated up all the more whitely. It was late at night. The wagon of a vendor who had closed shop moved off. At the firecracker stand, unwrapped firecracker sticks; Azuma Peonies; Flower Wheels; Land Mines wrapped in colored paper bags; Snow, Moon, and Flowers; and Three-Colored Pine Needles in colored paper boxes were lined up in red-ochre rows. At the optician's stall, old-age glasses; glasses for the nearsighted; tinted glasses; glasses for show with frames of gold (probably gilt), silver, gold and copper alloy, steel, or tortoiseshell; binoculars; dust goggles; swimming goggles; magnifying glasses; and the like were ranged in rows. But I wasn't looking at the firecrackers or the eyeglasses.

The firecracker stand and the optician's stall were about three feet apart. Since no one was looking at their goods, the two vendors had come out of their stalls and seemed to be doing something together in that three-foot space. If the glasses vendor had moved two feet into the space and the firecracker vendor one foot, it was only because the firecracker girl had shifted her shop bench, too, while the glasses vendor had left his bench behind his stall. He didn't seem to miss it.

Floating up on his toes, his legs slightly spread, the man pressed down hard on his left knee with the elbow to which he entrusted the weight of his bent-over upper body. With a girl's short bamboo clog, which he dangled between his legs from his right hand, he was busy writing characters in the black dirt.

The girl was intently reading, from the top down, the column of characters being written by the man. The bench on which she sat was low and her clogs had teeth so that her knees were raised and slightly parted. Her shop apron dangling between her legs, she bent over so that her small breasts pressed against her knees; her arms hung down around them, her hands resting lightly, palms upward, on her insteps. Her crudely patterned summer kimono was somewhat sweat-stained, and her "cleft-peach" coiffure had come slightly undone. Because of her breasts pressing against the slightly parted knees, the collar of her kimono clung to her nape and, in front, revealed a little of her bosom.

Observing these two and the ground being written on, I loitered nearby. Although I could take the pair in at a glance, I wasn't able to make out the characters inscribed by the clog. The man, not erasing a character once he had written it but simply writing over it, kept doing one after the other. Even so, the firecracker girl could probably read them. When some meaning had been completed there on the ground, without thinking to or knowing it, the two would suddenly raise their faces and glance at each other. But, before they could smile at each other or say something with their eyes or lips, the girl would drop her eyes to the ground and the man would start to write again. The girl had the slender fingers and waist of a child born to a poor family in old downtown Tokyo, but she seemed to have shot up ahead of her years.

When the man had written three or four new characters, the girl abruptly leaned forward off the bench. Reaching out her left hand, which had rested on her instep, she tried to snatch the clog away from the man. The man nimbly withdrew his hand. They exchanged glances. But neither said a word, and neither showed any change of expression. It was strange. The girl docilely brought her hand back to her instep. The man planted himself solidly on his heels, spread his knees farther apart, and began to write another character. This time, before he had finished the character, the girl shot out her left hand like lightning. But the man's hand was even quicker. Giving up, the firecracker girl again drew back her hand docilely. As she was returning her hand to her instep, she suddenly turned her face to the side and met my eye. I wasn't ready for such an encounter. Involuntarily, she flashed me a little smile. I, also involuntarily, gave her a little smile in return.

The firecracker girl's smile passed straight into my heart. As I watched the postures and actions of the couple, the smile that was in my heart was lured to the surface in all its purity by the girl. It was an innocent smile.

The man, drawn by the direction of the girl's gaze, also looked at me. Giving me a sly grin, he then immediately put on a stern face. Suddenly I felt chilled. The girl, blushing slightly, raised her left hand to her cleft-peach hairdo as if to tidy it. Her face was hidden by her sleeve. All of this had taken place in the short space of time after the girl had stretched out her hand to snatch the bamboo clog from the man. Although I lightly parried the ill will of the look he threw at me, I felt ashamed of having stolen other people's secrets. I walked away.

Glasses vendor! Your displeasure is understandable. Probably you did not know it, but the girl's blushing and hiding her face with her sleeve must have been on your account. Because a little smile that bloomed fleetingly outside the night stall was stolen from you by me. Of course, even though you glanced at each other, you were so intent on what you were doing that your faces were almost expressionless. So the girl's smile ought to have been given to you. If only I hadn't been looking, you probably would have given the girl the same smile in return. However, if I stole a glimpse and a moment of that time before the girl's father or older brother came for her, if my innocent smile at that instant mirrored the girl's own smile, didn't you in turn give me a hard look along with your sly smile? If I may use the terms of your trade, the spectacles of your heart are slightly clouded and out of focus. But there is tomorrow evening, and the evening after. Write down thousands, hundreds of thousands of characters in the dirt until you reach the center of the earth!

Firecracker girl! Left-handed girl! For you, it's probably all the same, but I worry that, as you peer down into the well that the glasses dealer, by writing thousands and hundreds of millions of characters, will carve into the earth with the bamboo clog, you may have a dizzy spell and fall down that well. I cannot tell whether it is better to fall down such a well or to guard against falling. Probably it would be best for you to follow behind the wagon that your father or older brother, who has come for you, draws behind him, thinking of the glasses dealer as you walk along the deserted streets of the neighborhood. . . . But how would it be if you were to set off all at once all of the firecrackers lined up in your stall—the Azuma Peonies, the Flower Wheels, the Land Mines, the Snow, Moon, and Flowers, the Three-Colored Pine Needles—making a flower of fire bloom in the lonely night? If you did that, even the glasses vendor might jump up in absolute astonishment and run away.

LD

The Blind Man and the Girl

[1928]

O-Kayo did not understand why a man who could return by himself on the Government Railway Line from this suburban station needed to be led by the hand along the straight street to the station. But, although she didn't understand, at some point or other it had become O-Kayo's duty. The first time Tamura had come to their house, her mother had said, "O-Kayo, please see him to the station."

A while after they had left the house, Tamura, shifting his long staff to his left hand, had groped for O-Kayo's hand. When she had seen his hand blindly swimming alongside her chest, O-Kayo, blushing scarlet, could not but hold out her own hand.

"Thank you. You're still a little girl," Tamura had said.

She'd thought she would have to help him onto the train, but Tamura, when he'd received his ticket and pressed a coin into her palm, briskly entered the ticket gate on his own. He made his way alongside the train, continually touching his hand to it at the height of the windows, toward the entrance, where he boarded. His movements had a practiced skill. O-Kayo, who'd been watching, felt relieved. When the train got under way, she could not hold back a little smile. It seemed to her there was a strange working virtue in his fingertips, as if they were his eyes.

There was also this kind of thing: By the window where the evening sunlight shone in, her older sister O-Toyo was repairing her ravaged makeup.

"Can you see what's reflected in this mirror?" she had said to Tamura.

The ill will of her sister's remark was clear even to O-Kayo. Wasn't it obvious that O-Toyo, redoing her makeup, was reflected in the mirror?

But O-Toyo's spitefulness simply came from being enamored of her own reflection. "A woman this beautiful is doing you the favor of being this nice to you," her voice implied as it coiled around Tamura.

When he'd silently crawled to her side from where he'd been sitting Japanese-style, Tamura began stroking the glass of the mirror with his fingertips. Then, with both hands, he wrenched the mirror stand around.

"Ah, what are you doing?"

"There's a forest reflected in it."

"A forest?"

As if lured by the mirror, O-Toyo slid over on her knees in front of it.

"The evening sun is shining through the forest."

O-Toyo looked dubiously at Tamura as he moved his fingertips around on the mirror's surface. Then, laughing with scorn, she returned the mirror stand to its place. Once again, she busied herself with her makeup.

But O-Kayo had been astonished by the forest in the mirror. Just as Tamura had said, the setting sun sent a smoky, purplish light through the high treetops in the forest. The broad, autumnal leaves, receiving the light from behind, glowed with a warm transparency. It was an intensely peaceful evening on a balmy autumn day. And yet the feeling of the forest in the mirror was completely different from that of a real forest. Perhaps because the delicate smokiness of the light, as if strained through silk gauze, was not reflected, there was a deep clear coldness about it. It was like a scene at the bottom of a lake. Although O-Kayo was used to seeing a real forest from the windows of her house every day, she had never looked at it attentively. Described by the blind man, it was as if she were seeing a forest for the first time. Could Tamura truly see that forest, she wondered. She wanted to ask him whether he knew the difference between a real forest and the forest in the mirror. His hand, stroking the mirror, became weird to her.

And so, when her hand was grasped by Tamura as she was seeing him off, it suddenly frightened her. But, since that was repeated as part of her duty each time Tamura came to the house, she even forgot about her fear.

"We're in front of the fruit store, aren't we?"

"Have we come as far as the undertaker's?"

"Is the dry-goods store still ahead?"

As they went along the same street time and again, Tamura, not altogether playful and not altogether serious, would often ask this kind of thing. On the right, the tobacconist's, the rickshaw stand, the footwear shop, the wicker-suitcase shop, the stall that served red bean soup with rice cakes; on the left, the sake dealer's, the Japanese sock dealer's, the buckwheat noodle stall, the sushi shop, the hardware store, the toiletries store, the dental clinic—just as O-Kayo had taught them to him, Tamura remembered the exact order of the shops along the six or seven blocks on the way to the station. It became his pastime to call out the shops one by one on either side as they went by. And so, when a new bit of wayside scenery came into being, such as a Japanese cabinetmaker's or a Western-style restaurant, O-Kayo would tell Tamura. Thinking that Tamura had hit on this sort of sad game to distract her, O-Kayo still found it strange that he should know the houses along the way just like a sighted person. But, without her knowing exactly when, the game had become a custom.

Once, though, when her mother was sick in bed, Tamura

had asked, "Are there artificial flowers today in the undertaker's window?"

As if she'd had water thrown over her, O-Kayo gave Tamura a startled look.

At another time, he had casually said, "Are your older sister's eyes all that beautiful?"

"Yes, they're beautiful."

"Are they more beautiful than anyone else's?"

O-Kayo was silent.

"Are they more beautiful than your eyes, Kayo-chan?"

"But how would you know?"

"How would I know, you say. Your sister's husband was blind. Ever since her husband's death, she has known only blind people. And your mother is blind. So naturally your sister has come to think that her eyes are extraordinarily beautiful."

For some reason, these words sank deep into O-Kayo's heart.

"The curse of blindness lasts three generations." O-Toyo, heaving a sigh, would often say that sort of thing in their mother's hearing. O-Toyo was afraid of giving birth to a blind person's child. Although the child itself might not be blind, she had the feeling that, if it was a girl, it would probably become the wife of a blind person. She herself had married a blind person because her own mother was blind. Her mother, associating only with blind masseurs, had dreaded the prospect of a sighted son-in-law. After O-Toyo's husband had died, many different men had stayed overnight at the house, but every single one of them was blind. One blind man passed the word on to another. The family had become imbued with the feeling that if they sold their bodies to any man who was not blind, they would be arrested immediately. It was as if the money to support the blind mother had to come from blind people.

One day, one of those blind masseurs had brought Tamura. Tamura, not of the fellowship of masseurs, was a wealthy young man who was said to have given several thousand yen to a school for the blind and deaf. Afterward, O-Toyo had made Tamura her only customer. She treated him as a complete fool. Tamura, always with a lonely air, would talk to the blind mother. At such times, O-Kayo would gaze quietly and earnestly at him.

Her mother had died of her illness.

"Now, Kayoko, we've escaped from the misfortune of blindness. We're in the clear," O-Toyo said.

Not long afterward, the cook from the Western-style restaurant walked into the house. O-Kayo shrank away in fear from his sighted person's uncouthness. Then the time came when O-Toyo parted from Tamura. For the last time, O-Kayo saw him off at the station. When the train pulled out, she felt a loneliness as if her life were over. Getting on the next train, she went after Tamura. She did not know where he lived, but she had a feeling that she would know which way a man whose hand she had held so many times would go.

LD

The Wife's Search

[1928]

Through the open windows of the Government Railway train came the scent of young leaves. The woman, clinging to the leather strap, let out a succession of sneezes. Her feet were planted, toes outward, in an indomitable stance—any way one looked at her, she was holding her ground. As she gripped the leather strap, an orange parasol dangling from her arm, her sleeves were swept back. Her hair, done in a low bun as if bunched up carelessly with one hand, exposed her blue, shaven nape, so that even from the back she seemed to be regarding him derisively. Her *haori*, of a simple emerald-striped pattern against a dark indigo ground, seemed in need of laundering. Her body bent at an angle toward the side with the parasol; her hipbones jutted out beneath the *haori*. It was all he could do not to rap the protuberance with his knuckles.

In this posture, the woman, lifting a perfunctory fist to her nose, was sneezing away. She was also emitting cavernous yawns. Asada burst out laughing. The woman seemed to have tumbled right out of her bed onto the train this May afternoon. Probably she thought the young foliage outside the train window was the young foliage outside her bedroom window. The woman was relaxed down to her bones. The green wind of May seemed to blow right through her body.

Asada, mocked at by the blue shaven eyes of the woman's nape, sat across from her in his neat university uniform. Although he knew that she was his older schoolmate Ando's wife, the lady probably wouldn't remember his face. Furthermore, if he offered her his seat, she might say some ridiculous thing and make him blush with embarrassment.

After the next station, he and Ando's wife were sitting right across from each other. He suddenly thought he would say hello to her. But, although she swiveled her eyes all around her as if in a panic, the woman did not seem to see anything. Bringing the short parasol onto her lap, she lightly placed it on her shoulder, just like a child with a toy gun. After that, oblivious of her surroundings, she let out another gaping yawn. Perhaps because her lips were extremely soft and rubbery, it was a startlingly round-mouthed yawn. Her teeth were beautifully regular, so as to make it seem that the yawn was meant to show off her lovely teeth. But the lady, insouciant as ever, blinking away the tears of sleepiness with a series of winks that one could almost hear—*pachi, pachi*—swabbing her moist eyeballs with the wipers of her eyelids, mischievously worked her eyes all about her.

Asada felt like shouting with laughter. He wanted somehow to startle this lady, who seemed to have forgotten such things as surprise and fear. And so, when she got off the train, he hurried after her.

"Mrs. Ando, isn't it? I'm Asada."

"Ah, yes."

"Just now, on the train . . ."

"Oh, were we on it together? I didn't see you. How rude of me."

"No, not at all. I was the rude one. I met you once on the Ginza with Mr. Ando. I recognized you right away."

"My, my, is that so?"

"It's strange. You look just like Mr. Ando's younger brother Shinkichi."

"Oh?"

Thinking, "I've surprised her," Asada let a sweet smile float up to his lips.

"You seem to have gradually come to resemble Shinkichi."

"Hmmm. I know my husband has a younger brother, but I've never met him. Can something like that really happen? Have you met the younger brother recently?"

"Yes, often."

This was a complete lie. He hadn't seen the brother in three or four years.

In Ando's study, on the worktable, there was a luxurious profusion of lilacs, like a white peacock's tail. The bookshelves, set into the wall, gave something of the feeling of an armoire. On the doors, in a refined Japanese-style scene, there was a scattering of autumn leaves in mother-of-pearl. Outside, the garden was a mass of flaming-scarlet azaleas.

Still in her street clothes, Ando's wife brought them some black tea. She had stolen Asada's smile.

"Mr. Asada says I've gradually come to resemble Mr. Shinkichi."

"What?"

Ando had turned paler than the lilacs. Putting on a know-nothing face, his wife left the room. Asada felt Ando's gaze burning into his forehead.

The next time he called, there was only a single yellow rose on Ando's worktable. The azaleas in the garden were dark with decay, like a demon's blood.

When Ando had left the room for a while, his wife came in.

"Mr. Asada, you said a terrible thing. Since then, it's been like the quiet before the storm in this house."

"The storm?"

"Yes."

"You're joking, aren't you?"

"If it's funny, you're not laughing very much."

"But—that was just something I made up and said casually."

"That's a lie."

"A lie, you say? That time on the train, you seemed to be looking down your nose at me, so I thought I would surprise you just once—"

"It's not good to be deceitful. My husband seems to believe what you said, so I can't not believe it. Because I don't know what Mr. Shinkichi looks like. Look—the last time you were here, up there . . ." The wife pointed to a picture of poppies.

"Before, there was a portrait of his father. As soon as you left, my husband took it down. I forget when it was, but my husband said once that his younger brother resembled their father more than he did. The landscape that he put up afterward was of the garden of a house from which you could see the ocean. There was a white bench by a flower bed. When I looked at the picture, I felt that I somehow remembered this garden, that I had sat on that bench. Might it not be the garden of Mr. Shinkichi's house? I thought. That was my fantasy. I wanted you to see that picture. Isn't there a flower bed surrounded by lawn in Mr. Shinkichi's garden, and aren't some low-growing red flowers—I don't know what kind they are—in full bloom there? Perhaps because he'd become aware of my feeling, my husband changed the picture again for this one of the poppies. And now I'm starting to wonder if there aren't some poppies in bloom at Mr. Shinkichi's house."

"But, I haven't even met Shinkichi in four years now, let alone gone to his house. To build up something like that out of a casual joke—it's the flower of delusion that blooms in the fertile soil of human boredom. Make your feelings into something a little fresher—"

"No. It's a fresh mystery."

Asada had been a classmate of Shinkichi's in upper school. Shinkichi had left home when he married a young country relative who'd been entrusted to his parents' care. All Asada knew for certain was that the girl had not been the fiancée of Shinkichi's elder brother Ando. Other than that, he did not know how things had been.

In the clear autumn weather, Asada's mother spent her time fretfully tidying up the garden. The powder from the wings of an ancient moth scattered dustily from the bulb of the electric lamp. While Asada was thinking about discarding the bush clover in the ornamental alcove, Ando's wife unexpectedly came to call, accompanied by a nurse for her baby.

In Asada's room, Ando's wife took the baby from the nurse's arms. The baby, swaddled in silk, was asleep.

"Mr. Asada, I want you to see this baby. It's my child. Please look at it and decide if it looks like Mr. Shinkichi or not."

"What are you saying?"

Shocked, he looked at the woman's face. Although her cheeks were somewhat hollow, her color was good. The skin at the corners of her eyes seemed vaguely ravaged. Her gaze was fastened single-mindedly on the baby in her lap.

"Don't look at me. I want you to look at this child."

"Madam, I haven't met Shinkichi in a long time. And—"

"Still trying to be deceitful—"

"This is absolutely absurd!"

"The storm has broken. I've been driven out of the house with my newborn baby. My husband thinks I saw Mr. Shinkichi in secret and that this is his baby—despite the fact that I've never met Mr. Shinkichi. But I also have the feeling that what my husband says is true, you know. Probably this child really does resemble Mr. Shinkichi. Does that mean I am in love with Mr. Shinkichi?"

"It doesn't resemble him at all. If you were living with Mr. Shinkichi, it might possibly come to resemble him. But—"

"That's enough of your lies." With this, the woman opened her eyes wide and looked sternly at Asada. Just then, the child, waking up, began to cry violently.

"Ah-ah, hush, hush." Rocking the child in her arms, the woman suddenly burst into tears. "Mother will find out who your true father is. Together, we'll set out in search of Father. Mr. Asada, we can join hands in this. Please take me to Mr. Shinkichi's place. Please take me there right away."

In the woman's straightforward gaze, Asada recollected Shinkichi as he had once known him. For the first time, he realized that both mother and child did resemble Shinkichi.

LD

Her Mother's Eye

[1928]

With a frightened expression, almost falling over himself, the innkeeper's three-year-old baby came running into my room. Snatching my pencil in its silver holder from the top of my writing table, he fled without a word.

After a while, the maid came in. "This pencil must belong to you," she said.

"Yes, it's mine, but I gave it to that child who was here."

"But the nursemaid had it."

"She must have taken it away from the child. She should have let him keep it."

The maid smiled. It turned out that the pencil had been found at the bottom of the nursemaid's wicker trunk. The trunk was full of stolen items. There was a guest's card case, the long underwear of the proprietress, the chambermaid's boxwood comb and topknot ornament, and five or six bank notes.

About half a month later, the maid said to me, "There's never been anything so embarrassing. That girl has disgraced us."

Evidently the nursemaid's kleptomania had kept on getting worse. With ready cash, she had been buying bolts of cloth, one after the other, that were much too expensive for one of her class, at the dry-goods store in the village. The store had secretly sent word to the inn. At the request of the proprietress, the maid had interrogated the girl.

"If you're going to talk that way, I'll go and tell madam myself." Saying this, the girl had flounced out of the room.

"It was as if she were saying, 'I'm not going to confess to a mere maid like you.' "

According to the maid's story, the nursemaid, sitting before the proprietress and innocently tilting her head, had announced the items one by one as she remembered them. Adding together what she had taken from guests and the front desk, it came to about one hundred fifty yen.

"She said that she'd made three or four kimonos and Japanese coats for herself, and after that she'd sent her mother to the hospital in an automobile."

When the head clerk took her home to her parents, they received her without any particular sign of displeasure.

Shortly after the beautiful nursemaid had gone, I left the inn myself. Behind the horse-drawn bus, an automobile came racing after us as if ripping through the green forests. The wagon made way for it. Right alongside, the automobile stopped short. The nursemaid, all gussied up, got out. Giving a cry of delight, she rushed over to the wagon.

"I'm so happy to have met you. I'm going with my mother to the doctor's in town. My poor mother's losing the sight in one of her eyes. Why don't you ride in our automobile? I'll take you to the station. It'll be all right."

I jumped down from the wagon. What a bright joy there was in the nursemaid's face.

In the window of the automobile, the bandage that covered her mother's eye was visible as a patch of white.

LD

Thunder in Autumn

[1928]

Our wedding ceremony was held in a hotel room to the sound of an old-style bamboo flute. It was early autumn, when the young girls returned from the sea and went walking about the town like fine chestnut horses. Suddenly, lightning flashed at the window and thunder crashed as if it would break up the ceremony. The face of my seventeen-year-old bride went ashen. She closed her eyes and began to droop like a wet flag.

"Close the window—and the curtain!"

After the ceremony had ended, the bride's father spoke. "The girl's fear of thunder may be an ancient curse." Then he told this story of a dutiful son from the old province of Tamba.

"Yoshida Shichizaemon of Haji village in Tamba's Amada County was so devoted to his parents that the feudal lord commended him for his filial piety and exempted him from paying land taxes. Anyway, Shichizaemon's mother had such a fear of thunder that she would faint even at the sound of a drum. So, whenever the thunder rumbled, Shichizaemon would come racing home regardless of where he was or what he was doing. In the summer he would not even go as far as the neighboring village. And that was not all. Even after his mother died, Shichizaemon would run to the cemetery and wrap his arms around her gravestone whenever he heard the sound of thunder.

"One night as Shichizaemon huddled over his mother's gravestone, embracing it during a storm, he was struck by lightning and died. The next morning the sky was clear and beautiful. But when one of the villagers tried to pry Shichizaemon's arm from the stone, it broke into pieces. His black charred body was a figure of ash that crumbled to bits wherever it was touched. Evidently it was a mistake to try to remove the dutiful Shichizaemon from his mother's headstone. One old woman picked up a finger that had fallen to the ground and slipped it into her sleeve. She bowed low as she spoke. 'I'm going to feed this to my thoughtless, negligent son.'

"Other villagers, too, began to pick up pieces of the body.

"Some of those ashes have been passed down through the generations as a family treasure. When I was a child my mother fed me some of them. I wonder if that is why I—and this girl, too—fear thunder."

"This girl, too"—I referred to my new wife as her father did—"you gave some to this girl, too?"

"No, somehow I neglected it. But, if your father would like to give her some, I'll send some in a package."

In our new home outside the city, four crickets jumped out from behind my bride's new bureau. The white coverlet had not yet been removed. My new bride had the early summer brilliance of a bouquet of lilacs. Then, once again, the violent thunder cracked as if the summer would destroy itself. As I held my cowering little bride, what I first felt through her skin was something within her that was a mother. Who could say I would not become a charred corpse when I embraced this warm, soft tombstone?

The lightning flashed. Thunder that seemed to turn our marriage bed into a deathbed rumbled above the roof.

"The curtain—close the curtain!"

JMH

Household

[1928]

The blindness I refer to here need not mean only blindness of the eyes.

Taking his blind wife by the hand, the man led her up to the hill to see a house for rent.

"What's that sound?"

"The wind in a bamboo grove."

"Of course. It's been so long since I've been out of the house, I'd forgotten what the rustle of bamboo leaves sounded like. . . . You know, the stairs in the house we live in now are so awfully narrow. When we first moved there, I couldn't quite get the knack of climbing them. Now, just when I feel I've gotten used to them, you tell me we're going to look at a new house again. A blind person knows all the nooks and crannies in her own house. She's as familiar with it as she is with her own body. To a seeing person, a house is dead, but to a blind person it's alive. It has a pulse. Now am I going to have to bump into the posts and trip over the threshold again in a new house?"

Dropping his wife's hand, the man opened the whitewashed gate.

"It feels dark, as though the trees have overgrown the garden. Winters will be cold from now on," she said.

"It's a Western-style house with gloomy walls and windows. There must have been Germans living here before. The nameplate says 'Liederman.' "

But when he pushed open the front door, the man stepped back, as if struck by a glaring light.

"This is wonderful! It's so bright! It may be nighttime in the garden, but inside the house it's like noon."

The yellow-and-vermillion striped wallpaper was dazzling, like the draperies of white and scarlet that are displayed at ceremonies. The deep red curtains glowed like colored electric lights.

"There's a sofa, a fireplace, a table and chairs, a bureau, an ornamental lamp—all the furniture is here. Would you look at that!" Almost knocking her over, he made her sit on the sofa. She waved her hands like a clumsy ice skater, bouncing like a spring.

"Hey, there's even a piano." He took her hand and pulled her to her feet. She sat at the small piano next to the fireplace, gingerly touching the keys as though they were something fearful.

"Listen. It works!" She began to play a simple melody, probably a song she had learned when she was a young girl and could still see.

He went to the study, where a big desk sat. And, next to the study, he discovered a bedroom with a double bed. Here again were stripes, vermillion and white—this time on a coarse blanket wrapped around a straw-stuffed bedroll. He jumped on top. It was soft and springy. His wife's playing began to sound more joyful. But he could also hear her laugh like a child when she occasionally missed a note—the sorrow of blindness.

"Come in here and look at this big bed."

It was uncanny, but the woman walked briskly through the strange house like a sighted girl all the way to the bedroom.

They hugged each other. He made her bounce like a jack-in-the-box as they sat on the bed. The woman began to whistle softly. They had forgotten the time.

"Where is this place?"
"Well . . ."
"Really, where is it?"
"Wherever it is, it's not your house anyway."
"How nice it would be if there were lots of places like this."

JMH

The Rainy Station

[1928]

Wives, wives, wives, wives—oh, women, how many of you, in this world, are called by the name of wife? I know it is not unusual for all girls to become men's wives, but, my friends, have you ever seen a large crowd of wives? It's a painful surprise, like seeing a crowd of prisoners.

You cannot imagine the difference between a crowd of wives and a crowd of girls' school students or female factory workers. The students or the workers are joined together by something they have in common. In brief, they have been liberated from their homes by that something. But a crowd of wives is made up of solitary individuals, who have come out from their respective homes as though from the isolation wards of this world. If it's a charity bazaar or a class reunion picnic, one might say that even wives become schoolgirls again for a short while. But such a gathering, occurring only because of the love of each wife for her husband, is likewise made up of solitary individuals. However, this is not a story about lonely crowds.

Let's take a suburban railway station—Omori, say. The clear autumnal skies have clouded over since noon, and it is raining, let's say. A writer is seeing off his wife. Since, unfortunately, she is not an isolation-ward patient but a taxi dancer in a hall in Shigeno, at the ticket gate an umbrella has been thrust at him by the neighbor's wife, with these words: "Get back nice and dry, now. I've brought you an umbrella."

What had been thrust at him was not merely an umbrella

but the feeling itself of "wife." Blushing right down to her neck, the neighbor's wife smiled at him. That was only natural. A big crowd of wives, each with two umbrellas, stood around the station exit ten and twenty deep, glaring with one accord at the ticket gate.

"Oh, thank you. It's like a May Day of housewives." He was even more flustered than the neighbor's wife. Like a madly excited orator, he fled down the stone stairs.

When he'd broken through the enclosure of women and stopped to get his breath, he heaved a sigh of relief and opened the umbrella. To his surprise, what he opened was a woman's umbrella, water green, with a design of big blue irises. Whether in her confusion she'd handed him the wrong umbrella or whether she'd brought her own umbrella for him, the gentle feelings of a woman who has come out to the station in the late-autumn rain soaked into his heart like water.

Often, from his second-floor study, he had gazed at the flesh above her ankles as, working the pump at the well, she had stood on tiptoes with the skirt of her kimono slightly open. When their eyes met, her smile had made him think of the autumn wind blowing on ripe-colored fruit. She was that kind of woman. But now, as he put up her flower-patterned umbrella and thought of his wife, dancing like crazy in the arms of one man after another, the old familiar loneliness came over him.

From the three main thoroughfares that converged on the station, an army of housewives, brandishing aloft in their umbrellas a domestic—an all-too-domestic—love, was charging to the attack. Their hurrying feet, their simple, artless air of weak health, unused to the outdoor light, their humility, made one think, on the contrary, of an angry attack by the downtrodden, the meek of the earth, the prisoners.

"The May Day of housewives—that was a good metaphor,

if I do say so myself." Moving against the tide, against the endless advance of wives, each carrying her husband's umbrella, he thought to himself, "These wives who have come out of their kitchens without putting any makeup on—they're exact images of their unmade-up households. It's an exhibition of the households of company employees."

He smiled a smile that was like the rainy autumn sky itself. But the wives of the rainy station were not smiling. There were even wives who, weary of waiting, were close to tears.

Actually, the neighbor's wife did not hand even the second umbrella to her husband.

Although these details will clearly expose the fact that the suburban neighborhoods of these rainy stations—for instance, Omori or thereabouts—are warrens of young married couples where the office-worker husbands do not ride in automobiles and the wives in their common silk kimonos do not have maids, I must admit that it is not at all unusual to see in the crowd housewives with coarse oiled-paper umbrellas, their babies strapped to their backs, old peasant women using their husbands' furled umbrellas as walking sticks, as well as young wives who, with no autumn raincoats, are wearing dark red woolen winter overcoats. . . . They of this gathering swarm of wives, wives, wives, once they have spotted their menfolk emerging from the ticket gate when the workday is done, return home together, umbrella alongside umbrella or perhaps under the same umbrella, with a feeling of relief and reassurance, a gladness and a delight peculiar to this one time of day, which brings back the joy of their honeymoon. And yet their numbers, continually pressing in around the station exit, put one in mind of a marketplace of the world's women in search of their spouses, the very model of a marriage marketplace, absolutely devoid of makeup and romance.

The neighbor's wife, however, was hoping that she would be the one and only article in this marketplace that remained unsold. She was in fear and trembling lest her poor husband should come through the ticket gate. For, when she'd handed the umbrella to the writer, her old rival in love had come up the stone stairs toward her.

"My, it's been a long time. Are you living in Omori, too?"

"Why, it's you." The two classmates smiled as if they'd just recognized each other.

"Wasn't that Mr. Nenami, the writer, just now?"

"Yes."

"Ah, so that's the way it is, is it? I'm jealous. When did you get married?"

"When, did you say . . . ?"

"What a strange person. You mean you've been so happily married you've forgotten the day of your own wedding?"

"It was last July," the wife suddenly asserted.

She had not brought the umbrella for the writer's sake. But, spotting her old rival at the station, she'd battled with her emotions. On the spur of the moment, she'd handed the umbrella to the successful writer Nenami.

"That's already more than a year, isn't it? You're blushing like someone who was married just yesterday."

"I'm glad I met you."

"I'm glad, too. You must let me visit you soon. I'm a passionate reader of Mr. Nenami. I'd read about what a handsome man he was in gossip columns, but he's even handsomer than they say. I'm jealous. Truth to tell, Chiyoko, I spotted you a while back. But, with things as they were, probably I would have just gone on my way. I didn't know whether to introduce myself or not. But when I realized that you were Mr. Nenami's wife, I felt free and easy. After all, as things have turned out, it's you who have drawn the lucky lottery ticket—thanks to my having drawn a losing one ahead of you. Instead of holding a grudge from the past, you should be thanking me. It's water under the bridge—water under the bridge, nothing! It's a bad dream that you've already completely forgotten about because you're happy now. When I realized we could be friends again the way we were, I felt lighthearted. I was beside myself, I was so happy. I wanted to congratulate you. So I came over to greet you."

You're lying. I've won. The neighbor's wife grew numb, paralyzed with happiness.

"Are you still waiting for somebody?"

"Yes, I've sent a woman disciple of his to do some shopping at the Matsuya." This time, her voice was cheerful and definite.

To employ once again Nenami's favorite metaphor, the ticket gate is like the gate of the enormous prison of society. The men, convicts serving a life sentence of penal servitude, come through that gate and, together with the invalids who have come to meet them, return home to their isolation wards. These, however, were two wives who dreaded their husbands' release from prison. Each time the train pulled in, they felt a cold shiver of fear in their hearts. Whose husband would arrive first?

The neighbor's wife loved her husband too much to go back to wearing the mask of being Nenami's wife. Just as her old rival had said, she *had* completely forgotten about that old love because of her love for the new. But to see her old flame being greeted by the rival no doubt would be as painful as having her mask ripped off. Still, the chains of habit, of coming to meet her husband, bound the wife to the rainy station on this autumn afternoon.

For her part, the rival did not want her husband, who was no longer the university student whom they both had loved, the handsome youth of the other woman's memories, but a low-paid office worker worn out by life, to be seen. Without so much as carfare in his pocket, his threadbare business suit the same one he'd worn at their wedding and in the four years since, soaked to the skin by the late autumn rain, her husband was no prize. But she could not just return home in defeat.

"Truly the skies of autumn mean a wife in tears. Today it's not so, but most days all the taxis are soon gone. So we're dragged out in a sort of loyalty-to-husbands contest. It's like a women's old-clothes market, isn't it?" Realizing she was no match for the other in this talk of husbands, the rival attacked the subject of solidarity. "Look at us, now. It's an accomplishment, no matter how shopworn our clothes are, to put on some light makeup and come to the station. It's the revolt of the women."

"My husband said it was the May Day of housewives."

"Ah, and well he might. That's how it is. We expose our husbands' shame, looking so awful."

Brightly dressed, down to her yellow-lacquered high clogs, the rival was wearing new makeup. Usually the neighbor's wife had come from her kitchen just as she was. Her rival did not forget to put on makeup even when it was just to meet her man at the rainy station with an umbrella—it was the kind of thing that in the past had stolen away the neighbor's wife's boyfriend. But now the neighbor's wife had put on the rouge of a writer husband, and she was happy because of that makeup. She had defeated her rival.

"But I have an inferiority complex. I'm afraid of attracting people's attention."

"That's your happy fate. Only a select few know that you're Mr. Nenami's wife. If you like, I'll noise it abroad for you. 'Allow me to introduce Mr. Nenami's wife,' I'll say," the other said, going further than the neighbor's wife would have liked her to. Then, as her third strategy, the rival began redoing her makeup. Meanwhile, airily, she brandished her connoisseurship in music and the "new theater."

Just then, his forehead rising above the soft felt hats of the office workers like a white flower, crossing the bridge over the tracks, who should be coming this way but that celebrated new-theater actor who lived in Omori. Having observed him come back late at night arm in arm with Nenami's dancer wife, the neighbor's wife also knew him by sight. He was the person with whom her old rival was rumored to be more than friends these days.

"Ah, it's Nakano Tokihiko." At this exclamation from the neighbor's wife, the made-up rival moved off briskly toward the ticket gate.

"Mr. Nakano, isn't it? I was waiting for you. Please come back with me under my umbrella as if we were lovers." Whispering this, the rival flirtatiously played up to him. It was her good luck that this Nakano, whom she was meeting for the first time, was an actor of lover's parts. Hiding the man's shoulder behind her umbrella, which she stylishly twirled open with one hand, she turned around.

"I'll lead the way." Triumphantly, she plunged into the sea of wives' umbrellas.

Like a field of bog rhubarbs in a gust of wind, the umbrellas in the plaza outside the station rustled and swayed with enmity toward this splendidly made-up pair. Instantly, the crowd became an organized crusade of honest women, the household brigade. But the neighbor's wife was still too intoxicated with her victory in makeup to join their number. That person may be the actor's lover, but she is not his wife. I am the wife of a famous writer. Even though they both had makeup on, hers, rather than a lover's makeup that would soon fade and discolor, was the natural-colored makeup of a faithful wife. So, of course, she would never betray her real husband. Under the umbrella, she would tell him about this skirmish at the rainy station. And, this very day, she would tell him, with tears in her eyes, the secret story of her old love. Thus, even when she got drunk on the victory of makeup, her thoughts were with her husband. And now that her enemy was gone, she could wait for him without a shadow in her heart.

But was the happiness of makeup like the fruit high up in a tree? The neighbor's wife was no female acrobat, used to scrambling up the tree of makeup like her enemy. Although, riding on her enemy's back, she'd pecked at the fruit of being a writer's wife, the enemy had flown away out of the treetop on loudly flapping wings of adultery. Unless someone gave her a hand, she could not get back down to the ground to join the crusade of honest women. Although she waited and waited, her husband did not come to rescue her. The wives, wives, wives, collecting their husbands, husbands, husbands, dispersed into the rainy dusk. The walls of the station became as cheerless as the walls of a ruin. The incessantly falling wintry rain stiffened her eyelids with cold. Her makeup completely raddled, the neighbor's wife felt a violent hunger. Less able than ever to get away from the station, she simply and earnestly waited for her husband, with a heightened nervous awareness, like an exile on the Island of Demons.

Finally, at nine o'clock, when she'd been waiting for five hours, there at the ticket gate, toward which she was drawn unawares like a lengthening shadow, was not her husband but her old love—in short, her enemy's husband. Rather than finding the strength to return to herself, she was swept away by the sadness that abruptly gushed up inside her. With the miserable weariness of one who has just come out of prison, the man descended the stone stairs, fretfully looking around for his wife. When the neighbor's wife, without a word, held out her umbrella over his head, her tears fell like evening rain. He understood nothing.

From the second floor of the house to which his dancer wife had not yet returned, the writer dubiously looked out at his neighbor's darkened house in the late wintry night rain. And these words of warning to the husbands, husbands, husbands of the world came into his mind:

"Oh, husbands, on days of afternoon rain, especially on evenings of late-autumn rain, hurry back to the stations where your wives are waiting. I cannot promise that a woman's heart, like a woman's umbrella, will not be handed to another man."

LD

At the Pawnshop

[1929]

In the frosted glass door, brightly lit by the reflection of the snow, the New Year's decorations of pine boughs cast their shadows. Showing off a new white shirt under his kimono, the son of the pawnbroker sat in the shop. This boy had lips as red as a made-up girl's, and the soft flesh round his neck had a girlish luster. The plain unfinished woodwork of the lattice doors, evidently changed at the end of the year, had the artificial brightness of a stage set. Through the open lattice doors, the visitor had exchanged New Year's greetings with the boy. That was why, calmly smiling all the while, they were now talking about high-interest money. At 10 percent interest per month, that was thirty yen on three hundred yen. . . .

"Well, then if you have fifteen hundred or two thousand yen, can't you live splendidly on the interest? It's strange why everybody doesn't become a moneylender."

"That's why it would be better if you didn't borrow money. The interest is deducted in advance, and, what with the commission and investigation expenses, you end up with much less than the loan's face value. And a loan on credit, with no collateral—that's difficult," said the boy.

"I'm in a pinch. If your family knows of a moneylender in the neighborhood, I'd appreciate an introduction."

"Well, now." Although the boy was smiling at him with girlish friendliness, his voice had the practiced deceitfulness of a wily usurer.

If I go on talking with him, he may say we'll lend you the money, the visitor thought. But this selfish, forlorn hope of his could not be revealed in so much as the expression on his face. He thought of his wife, waiting outside on the snowy road. Just then, startling him, the gate opened. But it was not his wife. It was a man.

Like one who has fallen ill on the road and barely made it home to die, the man swayed back and forth, clutching the glass door, which he'd slid shut. Rubbing along the wall with his shoulder jammed up against it, he grabbed at the latticework of the counter.

"It's my first time. I want you to lend me some money on this."

He showed the boy a pair of women's long underwear. Its muslin lining was excessively soiled from the woman's skin. The first visitor looked away. At the skirt of the man's kimono, his ancient flannel night-clothes peeked out. The teeth of his heavy sandals were clogged with snow and mud, and the thick thongs were very loose.

"If it's your first time, I can't accept the item until I've made a visit to your house."

"Hmm. Actually, once before this, at the end of the year, I came and was told the same thing. That time, my wife felt ashamed because of the neighbors. But now my wife says we're beyond such things as shame and reputation, and that it's all right for you to come. Since November, the two of us haven't left our beds. I've come all the way from beyond the station like this. I may not be able to make it back. I can only walk very slowly. But if I have you come back with me, can you lend us a yen and fifty sen?"

"It's New Year's. I don't have anyone I can send."

"Please remember that I'm a sick man. It's taken me an

hour to travel barely a mile." The man broke off, coughing into a piece of newspaper. His knees were held tightly together in a formal sitting position. His dirty fingers, along with the newspaper, were trembling. In an arrogant, hectoring voice, as if he were dressing the boy down, he began to recite his miseries all over again. But the boy, like an obstinate young girl, said nothing.

"Still, you—" Grabbing the long underwear, the man began to wrap it up in the newspaper. Hurriedly concealing in his lap that part of the newspaper sprayed with blood, he barked, "Do you have blood in your veins? Huh? Human blood?"

"I'm sorry. I don't have so much that I can afford to cough any of it up."

"What!" With a violent cough, the man sprayed blood and saliva all over the latticework. "That's the blood of a human being. You just remember that."

The blue veins bulged in the man's forehead. His eyes rolled, and he seemed ready to collapse. The first visitor cut in.

"Excuse me. If one yen and fifty sen is all right, I'll lend it to you."

Surprised, the man looked at him. And then the strength seemed to go out of him. As the man hesitated, the gate opened again. The first visitor pressed the money into the sick man's hand.

"Please accept this." The man tried to give him the long underwear. When he refused, smiling, the man, hanging his head so low that his long hair tumbled forward, muttered something and staggered out of the shop. Bringing some disinfectant from an inner room, the boy wiped the blood off the latticework.

"It's as if he had come out of hell to blackmail you."

"How could I accept something that was like a nest of tuberculosis germs? And talking in that high-handed way, like a stage villain. I bet he's a Communist."

A new customer, who had entered the shop as if being pursued, stood in a corner, without trying to listen to their conversation. But, when the boy returned to the counter, he briskly came forward. Taking out of his kimono a small parcel wrapped in paper, he handed it to the boy.

"How much is it?" When the boy opened the packet, it was a bundle of bank notes. In order to hide the boy from the other visitor's eyes as he counted out the money, the man held the latticework so that his sleeves spread across it like a bat's wings. It was the same latticework that had just been wiped clean of blood. From behind, the man's batlike figure was both shabby and ominous. When he'd received his pawn ticket from the boy, he slouched out of the shop with the unsociability of a man living in the shadow of hardship.

"That was more than a hundred yen he had there. What on earth does he have in hock that he has to pay more than a hundred yen in interest?"

"It's not interest." The boy had finally recovered his girlish smile. "It's a secret, but that guy is pawning his capital."

"Is he a thief? Which of you is paying interest?"

"He's paying it, just the same as on an article. He says it's on account of his neighbors. He wants to make them think his house is always going to the pawnbroker's so they must be hard up. He's the exact opposite of that other man."

"If it's necessary for him to seem as poor as all that, the money must be tainted. What's his business?"

"If he's thought to be poor, he doesn't have to spend a lot of money. And people don't come to him for money."

"Well, now, I have people coming to me for money, and I don't know what to do. Why don't you lend me that strange money?"

"Well, now." The boy vanished into the interior of the house. Then, just as friendly as a young girl, he came running out again.

"The old man says it's all right. It's half of the three hundred yen you mentioned before."

The visitor skipped out of the shop into the sunlit snow. Standing among the children who were building a snowman at the edge of the forest, his wife smiled brightly and playfully at him.

LD

Lavatory Buddhahood

[1929]

One spring long, long ago in Arashiyama in Kyoto.

Ladies of the great Kyoto families, their daughters, geisha from the pleasure quarters, and prostitutes came in their spring finery to view the cherry blossoms.

"I'm so sorry to ask, but may I use your lavatory?" Women would bow, red-faced, at the gate of an unsightly farmhouse. When they went around to the back, they found the privy old and dirty with straw mats hanging around it. Every time the spring breeze blew, the Kyoto women's skin would crawl. They could hear children crying somewhere.

Seeing the distress of the Kyoto women, a peasant devised a plan. He built a tidy little privy and hung out a sign painted in black ink: "Pay toilet, three *mon*." During the flower-viewing season it was a huge success and he became a rich man.

"Lately, Hachihei has made a remarkable amount of money with his pay toilet. I think I'll build a privy next spring and knock off his business. How would that be?" one of the villagers, envious of Hachihei, said to his wife.

"That would be bad judgment on your part. You might build a privy, but Hachihei is the established business and has a clientele. You would be the newcomer. When yours didn't catch on, you'd be all the poorer."

"What you're missing is that the privy I'm thinking of wouldn't be filthy like Hachihei's. I've heard that the tea ceremony is popular in the capital, so I intend to build a privy after the style of a tearoom. First of all, for the four pillars, Yoshino logs would be dirty, so I'd use Kitayama knotwood. The ceiling would be bulrush, and I'd use a kettle chain in place of a rope. An ingenious idea, don't you think? I'd put windows in below ground level. And the planks will be of zelkova wood. The walls will be double-coated plaster, and the door will be of cypress. I'll shingle the roof with cedar and use Kurama stone for the step. Around it, I'll have a trellis with bamboo and beside the stone washbasin I'll plant a red pine. I'll build it to attract the Senke, Enshū, Uraku, Hayami, and all other schools of the tea ceremony."

The man's wife listened with a vacant air, then asked, "And how much will you charge?"

Somehow the man managed, through much tribulation, to build a splendid privy in time for the cherry blossom season. He had a priest paint the sign in showy T'ang style.

"Pay toilet, eight *mon.*"

The women of the capital merely gazed longingly at the privy, thinking it was just too beautiful to use. The man's wife pounded the floor. "Did you see that? That's why I said not to do it. You put all that money into it, and now what's going to happen?"

"There's nothing for you to get in such a huff about. Tomorrow when I go around soliciting, customers will gather like a line of ants. You get up early too, and fix me a lunch. I'll make some rounds and people will gather as though it's a village fair."

The man calmed down. But the next day he slept later than usual, waking about eight o'clock. He tucked up his kimono and hung his lunchbox around his neck. Then he looked back at his wife, grinning with sadness in his eyes.

"Well, Mother, you said this was a dream, a foolish dream.

Today you'll see. Once I make my rounds they'll come in droves. If the pot gets full, put up the closed sign and have Jirōhei next door dip out a couple of loads."

The man's wife thought it all terribly strange. "Make rounds," he had said. Was he planning to walk about the capital shouting, "Pay toilet! Pay toilet!"? As she was wondering, a girl soon came who tossed eight *mon* into the money box and entered the privy. After that, one after another, the customers never quit coming. The man's wife was baffled and wide-eyed as she tended the cash. Soon she put up the closed sign and there was a commotion as the pot was emptied. Before the day ended she had taken in eight *kan* and emptied the pot five times.

"My husband must be a reincarnation of the Bodhisattva Monju. It's the first time his dreams have come true."

Pleased, the man's wife bought some wine and was waiting for him when, pathetically, her husband's dead body was carried to their home.

"He died in Hachihei's pay toilet, from lumbago, it seems."

As soon as the man had left his own house that morning he had paid his three *mon*, gone into Hachihei's privy, and latched the door. Whenever anyone tried to come in, he cleared his throat. This continued until he grew hoarse and at the end of the long spring day he could not stand up.

The people of the capital heard the story.

"What a ruin for such a refined man!"

"He was an unrivaled master."

"The most stylish suicide ever in Japan."

"Lavatory Buddhahood! Hail, Amida Buddha!"

There were few who did not chant these words.

JMH

The Man Who Did Not Smile

[1929]

The sky had turned a deep shade; it looked like the surface of a beautiful celadon porcelain piece. From my bed I gazed out on the Kamo River where the water was tinged with the color of morning.

For a week now, filming for the movie had continued through the middle of the night because the actor playing the lead role was scheduled to appear onstage in ten days. I was merely the author, so all I had to do was casually witness the filming. But my lips had grown chapped, and I was so tired that I could not keep my eyes open, even as I stood next to the burning white carbide lamps. I had returned to my hotel room that morning about the time the stars were beginning to disappear.

However, the celadon-colored sky refreshed me. I felt that some beautiful daydream was about to take shape.

First, the scenery of Shijō Street came to mind. The previous day I had eaten lunch at Kikusui, a Western-style restaurant near Ōhashi. The mountains appeared before my eyes. I could see the new green of the trees of Higashiyama outside the third-story window. That was to be expected, but for me, having just come from Tokyo, it was startlingly fresh. Next, I recalled a mask I had seen in the display window of a curio shop. It was an old smiling mask.

"I have it. I've found a beautiful daydream," I whispered, overjoyed, as I drew some blank manuscript paper toward me and gathered the daydream into words. I rewrote the last scene of the movie script. When I had finished, I added a letter to the director.

"I shall make the last scene a daydream. Gentle smiling masks will appear all over the screen. Since I could not hope to show a bright smile at the end of this dark story, at least I could wrap reality in a beautiful, smiling mask."

I took the manuscript to the studio. The only thing at the office was the morning paper. The cafeteria woman was cleaning up sawdust in front of the prop room.

"Would you please leave this at the director's bedside?"

This movie took place at a mental hospital. It pained me to see the wretched lives of the insane people we filmed every day. I had begun to think that I would feel hopeless unless I could somehow add a bright ending. I was afraid that I could not find a happy ending because my own personality was too gloomy.

So I was elated that I had thought of the masks. I had a pleasant sensation when I imagined having every last person in the mental hospital wear a laughing mask.

The glass roof of the studio shone green. The color of the sky had lightened with the daylight. Relieved, I went back to my lodging and slept soundly.

The man who had gone to buy the masks returned to the studio about eleven o'clock that night.

"I've been running around to all the toy stores in Kyoto since morning, but there aren't any good masks anywhere."

"Let me see what you've got."

I was disappointed when I unwrapped the package. "This? Well . . ."

"I know. They won't do. I thought I'd be able to find masks just anywhere. I'm sure I've seen them at all kinds of shops, but this is the only thing I could come up with the whole day."

"What I envisioned was something like a Noh mask. If the mask itself isn't artistic, it will simply look ridiculous on film." I felt as though I might cry as I took the child's paper clown-mask in my hand. "For one thing, this color would look like faded black when photographed. And if it doesn't have a gentler smile with a whitish luster on the skin, then . . ."

The red tongue stuck out from the brown face.

"They're trying white paint on it now in the office."

Filming had stopped temporarily, so the director, too, came out of the hospital-room set, stared at everyone, and laughed. There was no way to collect enough masks; they had to shoot the last scene the next day. If they could not get old masks, he wanted at least to have celluloid ones.

"If there aren't any artistic masks, then we'd better give up," a man from the script department said, perhaps sympathizing with my disappointment. "Shall we go out looking one last time? It's only eleven o'clock, so they'll probably still be awake in Kyōgoku."

"Would you?"

We hurried by car straight along the dikes of the Kamo River. The bright lights in the windows of the university hospital on the opposite bank reflected in the water. I could not imagine that there were many patients suffering in a hospital with all those beautifully illuminated windows. I wondered if we might show the lights in the hospital windows instead, if we could not find suitable masks.

We walked around to each of the toy shops in Shinkyōgoku as they were beginning to close. We knew it was hopeless.

We bought twenty paper turtle-masks. They were cute, but they could hardly be called artistic. Shijō Street was already asleep.

"Wait a moment." The script man turned down an alley. "There are a lot of shops here that sell old Buddhist altar fittings. I think they have Noh theater equipment, too."

But no one was awake on the street. I peeped inside at the shops through the doors.

"I'll come again tomorrow morning about seven. I'll be up all night tonight anyway."

"I'll come along, too. Please wake me up," I said. But the next day he went alone. When I woke up, they had already started filming the masks. They had found five masks used in ancient music performances. My idea was to use twenty or thirty of the same kind of mask, but, touched by what it would be like to be floating in the gentle smiles of those five masks, I relaxed. I felt I had fulfilled my responsibility to the insane.

"I rented them because they were too expensive to buy. If you get them dirty, they can't be returned, so be careful."

After the script man spoke, the actors all washed their hands and picked up the masks with their fingertips, gazing at them as if viewing a treasure.

"If they were washed, the paint would peel, wouldn't it?"

"Well, then, I'll buy them." I did actually want them. I day-dreamed as if awaiting the future when the world would be in harmony and people would all wear the same gentle face as these masks.

As soon as I got back home to Tokyo, I went straight to my wife's hospital room.

The children laughed with joy, putting on one mask after another. I felt a vague sense of satisfaction.

"Daddy, put one on."

"No."

"Please put one on."

"No."

"Put one on."

My second son stood up and tried to push the mask onto my face.

"Stop it!" I shouted.

My wife saved me from this awkward moment. "Here, I'll put one on."

In the midst of the children's laughter, I turned pale. "What are you doing? You're ill."

How horrifying it was to see this laughing mask lying in her sickbed!

When my wife took off the mask, her breathing became labored. But that was not what horrified me. The moment she removed the mask, my wife's face somehow appeared ugly. My skin grew clammy as I gazed at her haggard face. I was shocked at having discovered my wife's face for the first time. She had been enclosed for three minutes in the beautiful, gentle, smiling expression of the mask, so now I was able to perceive the ugliness of her own countenance for the first time. But no, rather than ugliness, it was the pained expression of one crushed by misfortune. After it had been hidden by the beautiful mask, her face had revealed this shadow of a wretched life.

"Daddy, put it on."

"It's Daddy's turn now." The children pressed me again.

"No." I stood up. If I were to put on the mask, then take it off again, I would look like an ugly demon to my wife. I was afraid of the beautiful mask. And that fear aroused in me suspicions that the ever-smiling gentle face of my wife might itself be a mask or that my wife's smile might be artifice, just like the mask.

The mask is no good. Art is no good.

I wrote a telegram to send to the studio in Kyoto.

"Cut the mask scene."

Then I tore the telegram to shreds.

JMH

Samurai Descendant

[1929]

In the afternoon quiet, with the swaying treetops of the June forest reflected in his bathtub, he was listening to the voices from the women's bath. It was the typical chatter of the moment when each woman was showing off her baby, held against her froglike belly.

"This child, you know, ma'am, he doesn't like little toys. When he starts to walk before long, he'll kick up a fuss unless we move to a bigger house, I was telling my husband."

"How remarkable. Little boy, if you turn your house into a toy, you'll be like a goblin. Please be a greater hero than Yanagawa Shohachi."

"Yes, but, ma'am, today is the age of education—"

"Oh, you don't say. This little man here is very strange. He likes newspapers and picturebooks. When I give him picturebooks and newspapers, he looks at them quietly for ever so long."

"My, how impressive. This child, ma'am, he eats things like newspapers. He even tears up picturebooks and eats them. He puts everything in his mouth. I'm at my wit's end."

"Well, this little man never does anything like putting things in his mouth."

"My, he's so pretty. He looks like a baby who doesn't like to eat at all."

And then the women laughed that shrill woman's laughter, which sounds friendly but reveals nothing.

On his way out of the bathhouse, he glanced in at the women's bath. In the mirror of the dressing room, breasts like dead octopuses and babies' heads, like those breasts, jiggled unsteadily.

Typical of a clear interval in the rainy season, a pile of gravel was drying off by the wet roadside. On top of the pile, a fair-skinned girl drew the drawing board on her lap close to her chest when she saw him.

"He's the artist from over there," she whispered to the girls beside her as she blushed and pointed toward his studio. Caught by her coyness, he peered at the drawing board clasped to the girl's chest. On it was a watercolor of the thatched-roof cottage just across the way. But, rather than look at the color of the thatched roof, he looked at the color of the girl's gently swelling breasts inside her loose-fitting summer clothes. Her bare legs were stretched out on the gravel like flower stalks.

"You'll show your drawing to the artist." As he said this, he put his hand on the drawing board. Unexpectedly, it fell away from her chest easily. The girl gave a sharp scream.

"Mother!"

Startled, he turned around. The woman who had been holding up her baby in the bath a while before was standing at the gate of the house across the way. The girl, not looking at the mother whom she'd called to, abruptly got to her feet as he hesitated. It was as if a white flower had been thrust at him. Peeping at the watercolor in his hand, she slid down the pile of gravel. The mother vanished into the house. The other girls also stood up, awaiting his criticism of the painting.

"Is that your house over there?"

"Yes, it is."

"Your little brother is the youngest newspaper reader in the world."

The girl tilted her head like a swallow. Smiling gently, he showered her with more sarcasm. "Your place is the residence of samurai descendants. That's quite remarkable."

On his way to and from the bathhouse, he had formed the habit of looking up at the unusual nameplate outside the girl's house. "Okiyama Kanetake, Descendant of Samurai of the Daté Clan." When he thought of the man who still took the trouble to post such a notice outside this shabby rented house in a Tokyo suburb, he could not repress a wry smile. All that came to mind when he thought of the Daté clan was a movie called *Yanagawa Shohachi*, which he'd gone to see as a diversion in a country hot-spring town. When he realized that the woman in the bath who had told the little boy to become a greater hero than Yanagawa Shohachi was the wife of the samurai descendant, he felt like slapping his knee and laughing out loud. From the story of the baby who looked at newspapers and picture-books, the life of this family that declared itself to be descended from samurai appeared vividly to him. But perhaps the samurai descendant's wife knew no more about her husband's clan than that one name of the storybook hero. And didn't this girl in the casual Western dress come flying out of the house with the grandiose nameplate just like any swallow? Swallows don't understand sarcasm.

"The colors are good, but be a little freer with your line. Don't paint like a samurai descendant."

For example, a line like that of your leg, bare to the thigh, he wanted to say. At this third sarcasm, too, the girl only smiled, looking more and more like a white flower.

"If you like pictures, come to my place. I have all sorts of books of pictures."

"Can we go right now?"

When he nodded, the girl put on a determined look and followed briskly behind him. Whistling a carefree song to cover his "Aha!" smile, he walked along looking at his own feet. This girl, too, he'd suddenly realized, was a samurai descendant. Gathering the lowly neighborhood girls around while she painted a watercolor; flirting with him, the artist; calling out to her mother; leaving her companions behind and coming alone to his house—she did all these things because she wanted to feel that she, too, descended from a samurai.

Dropping his palm onto the girl's shoulder as if striking her, putting strength into his fingers as if to crumple up this samurai descendant, he said, "I'll do your portrait."

"Oh, that makes me so happy! You really will?"

"I really will. Today I'll just draw you in that white dress, but you must know from having gone to exhibitions that an artist can't draw the human body unless it's naked. Unless you're naked, I can't draw your true beauty. Next time, will you pose naked for me?"

The girl nodded, her face, like a bride's, tensing in submission. He felt as surprised as if he'd been pierced by a pin.

However, this also seemed to be the excessive bravery of a samurai descendant. Why? Because when he was alone with the girl in the studio, he began to feel the morality of the samurai within himself—although, like the baby who ate newspapers, he wanted to sink his teeth into her flesh and devour her, from her flower-stalk legs up, this samurai girl.

LD

The Rooster and the Dancing Girl

[1930]

Of course, the dancing girl hated it—carrying a rooster under her arm—no matter how late at night it was.

The dancing girl was not raising chickens. Her mother was raising them.

If the girl were to become a great dancer, perhaps her mother would no longer raise chickens.

"They're doing gymnastics naked on top of the roof."

Her mother was taken aback.

"Not just one or two. There are forty or fifty. Just like at a girls' school. Naked . . . well, their legs are."

The spring light overflowed from the concrete rooftop. The dancing girls felt their arms and legs stretching like young bamboo shoots.

"Even in elementary school they don't do gymnastics on the ground anymore."

The girl's mother had come to the door of the dressing room to see her daughter.

"The rooster crowed in the night. That's why I came. I thought something had happened to you."

Her mother waited outside until rehearsal was over.

"Starting tomorrow, I'm going to dance naked in front of an

audience." She had not told her mother before. "There was a strange man here. The dressing room bath was right by where you were waiting. Someone said there was a man who stood there vacantly watching for an hour—even though the window was up high and made of frosted glass. He couldn't even see a shadow. They said he just watched the drops that formed on the glass as they ran down the window."

"No wonder the rooster crowed at night."

There was a custom of discarding roosters that crowed at night to the deity Kannon of Asakusa. By doing so, they say you could avoid calamity.

Evidently the chickens that lived among the Kannon's pigeons were all faithful prophets for their masters.

The dancing girl went home once the next evening, then went back to Asakusa, crossing Kototoi Bridge from Honjo. She was carrying a rooster wrapped in cloth under her arm.

She untied the bundle in front of the Kannon. As soon as the rooster touched the ground, it flapped its wings and hurried away.

"Chickens are real idiots."

She felt pity for the rooster, which was probably cowering in the shadows. She looked for it but could not find it.

Then the dancing girl recalled that she had been told to pray.

"Kannon, did you once dance long ago?" She bowed her head. When she looked up again, she was startled.

She gazed at the high branches of a gingko tree and saw four or five chickens roosting there.

"I wonder how that rooster is doing."

On the way to the theater, the dancing girl stopped in front of the Kannon.

The rooster she had delivered the day before began to approach her. Blushing, the girl fled. The rooster chased after her.

The people in the park stared, their mouths gaping open as the rooster chased the girl.

Day by day the rooster became a wild bird among the crowds of people in the park.

It began to fly well. Its wings were covered with dust and turned white. But it pecked at beans alongside the pigeons with the nonchalance of an Asakusa delinquent and swaggered about on top of the offertory chest of the deity.

The dancing girl never tried to pass in front of the Kannon again.

Even if she *had* passed by, the rooster had forgotten her.

At the dancing girl's house, twenty chicks had hatched.

"It's probably not an ill omen for chicks to peep at night."

"For humans, you know, it's only natural for a child to cry at night."

"It's strange for an adult to cry at night."

The dancing girl spoke these trivial words; still, she had begun to feel that they had meaning.

She often walked with boys who were students. It seems that dancing girls who were not particularly great sometimes walked with students.

When she got home, her mother said, "I wonder what can be the matter. A rooster crowed at night again. You go pray to the Kannon."

The dancing girl felt she had been discovered, but she smiled. "Twenty chicks have hatched, so maybe the rooster's crowing means it's all right for me to walk with twenty men. That would be enough for one lifetime."

But she was mistaken. The rooster's prophecy was not about walking with students.

A strange man followed the dancing girl as she carried the rooster in a bundle under her arm. But because of the rooster, the girl was more embarrassed than afraid. Then the timid girl—that's right—we should shout to warn her.

A dancing girl carrying a rooster was certainly a bizarre sight. The man surely thought this would be convenient.

"Young lady, wouldn't you like to take part in a fine money-making plan with me? I search through the trash can every day at the theater where you dance—not to pick up scraps or anything like that. The trash is full of love letters addressed to the dancers, ones that they've thrown away."

"Oh?"

"You catch what I'm getting at, don't you? We could use those letters to get a little money from the men who were fools enough to send them. If I had someone in the dance hall who would assist me, it would make the work that much easier."

The dancing girl tried to run away. The man grabbed her. Without thinking, the girl pushed his face to the side with her right hand—the hand that held the rooster.

She shoved the bundle, rooster and all, into the man's face. The rooster flapped its wings. How could he stand it?

The man fled, screaming. He did not know it was the rooster.

The next morning, when the girl tried to walk in front of the Kannon, wouldn't you know it but the rooster from the previous night was there and came running to her feet. She stifled a laugh, but this time she did not run away. She left quietly.

As soon as she entered the dressing room, she said, "Everyone, please take care of your letters. Let's not throw them in the trash can. And let's send a notice to the other theaters—to protect public morals."

Of course, with this, perhaps she *would* become a great dancing girl.

JMH

Makeup

[1930]

My bathroom window faces the restroom of the Yanaka Funeral Hall. The narrow space between the buildings is the funeral hall's trash dump where they dispose of funeral wreaths and flowers.

The cry of the autumn insects had already grown loud in the graveyard of the funeral hall although it was only the middle of September. I put my hand on my wife's shoulder and led her and her younger sister down the hallway to show them something. It was night. As I opened the door of the bathroom at the end of the hall, the powerful fragrance of chrysanthemums struck us. Surprised, they leaned toward the window over the washbasin. The window was blooming with white chrysanthemums. About twenty wreaths stood in a row, left over from a funeral. As my wife reached out as if to take a flower, she wondered out loud how many years it had been since she had seen so many chrysanthemums at one time.

I turned on the light. The silver wrapping paper of the wreaths sparkled. While I was working that night, time and again I caught the scent of chrysanthemums when I went to the bathroom, and, each time, I felt the weariness of working all night vanish in the fragrance. Finally, in the light of day, the white flowers seemed all the whiter and the silver paper began to glow. As I tended to my business, I noticed a canary perched on the flowers. It was probably a bird released at yesterday's funeral ceremony that had gotten tired and had forgotten to return to the bird shop.

Although this was a beautiful sight, from my bathroom window I also have to look at the funeral flowers on other days as they rot away. Even now at the beginning of March, as I write this, I have been watching a wreath of bellflowers and red roses for four or five days, wondering just how the colors will change as they wither.

I wish the flowers were on living plants.

I also have to look at human beings in the window of the funeral hall restroom. There are a lot of young women. Few men seem to go into the restroom, and the longer the old women stay there the less they look like women. Most of the young women stand there for a moment, then do their makeup. When I see these women in mourning clothes doing their faces in the restroom, putting on dark lipstick, I shudder and flinch as if I've seen the bloody lips of one who has licked a corpse. All of them are calm and collected. Their bodies exhibit a sense of sin, as though they were committing some evil deed while they hid themselves.

I do not want to see such horrible makeup, but the windows face each other all year long, so such disgusting incidents are not at all rare. I always hurriedly look away. I think I may send letters to the women I like, telling them not to go into the restroom at the Yanaka Funeral Hall, even if they should come for a funeral—in order to keep them away from those witches.

Anyway, the other day I saw a girl of about seventeen or eighteen in the window of the restroom, drying her tears with a white handkerchief. Though she wiped her eyes again and again, still the tears overflowed. Her shoulders trembled as she sobbed. Finally, gripped by sorrow, she leaned against the wall. She gave in to her tears without the strength to dry her cheeks.

She was the only one who had come not to hide and put on her makeup. She had surely come to hide herself and cry.

The ill feelings toward women that had grown in me from looking through that window were washed clean by this girl. But then, unexpectedly, the girl took out a small mirror, gave a quick smile, and hurriedly left the restroom. I was so surprised, I felt as though someone had hit me with cold water. I almost called out to her.

It was a puzzling smile.

JMH

The Bound Husband

[1930]

Certainly there's no doubt that husbands are bound to their wives.

And yet it also happens sometimes that a husband is literally bound, hand or foot, by strings or cords or what have you, to his wife. For instance, when the wife is ill and cannot leave her bed and the husband is taking care of her—it tires the sick person to raise her voice sufficiently to rouse the sleeping husband. Perhaps, too, the wife is sleeping by herself and the husband in his own bed. How is the wife to get the husband up in the middle of the night? The best way is to tie a string to the husband's arm and, when the time comes, to give it a yank.

A wife sick in bed is a lonely person. Say that the wind has blown down the leaves from the tree, or that she's had a bad dream, or that the mice are making a racket, she will get the husband up on some pretext or other to talk to him. The very fact that he is slumbering away at her sleepless side annoys her.

"Lately, you haven't been getting up when I pull on the string. I want to attach a bell to the string—a silver bell." She will think up this kind of pleasant game. And so, deep in the autumn night, say, what a melancholy music it is, the sound of that bell by which the bedridden wife rouses her husband.

Now, it was true that Ranko also bound her husband by means of a string around his leg. But she was the woman of a lively music, exactly the opposite from the melancholy music of the ailing wife's bell. She was a revue dancer. As the autumn grew colder, on her way from the dressing room to the stage, Ranko would get goose pimples on her naked, powdered flesh, but the jazz dancing would soon soak her makeup with sweat. Who, gazing at her legs, dancing away as if they had a life of their own, could have imagined that they were bound to a single husband? Actually, the husband had not bound her legs; rather, she had bound one of her husband's legs.

It was ten o'clock by the time the theater closed and she entered the dressing room bath. Only four nights out of ten was she able to get back to the apartment before the after-bath chill. The other six nights, rehearsals went on until two o'clock, three o'clock, until daybreak. Even though her apartment house, near Asakusa Park, had many theatrical tenants, it shut its doors at one o'clock.

"I have a string hanging down from my room on the third floor." Ranko thoughtlessly let this remark slip from her, one night in the dressing room. "The string's tied to that person's leg. When I pull on it from below, he gives a grunt and gets up."

"Aha. A real stringer, isn't he?"

(In the theatrical world, a man who lives off a woman is called a "stringer.")

"Ranko-san, you've said a terrible thing. It's dangerous. For instance, what if I went and pulled on the string? That person, because he was all sleepy, would think, 'It's Ranko-san,' and open the door. Even if I went up to the third floor, he might not notice it was the wrong person. I'm going over there right now to give it a try. Thanks for telling me."

If the banter had been confined to the dressing room, that would have been well and good. However, the secret of the string reached the ears of a band of juvenile delinquents who frequented the theater. Getting hold of complimentary tickets from somewhere, they would sit together in a clump in the balcony and make it their business to yell out the names of the dancers onstage. They talked of going to pull on Ranko's string.

"Tonight, some of those shop-boy scamps may come over and pull on the string. . . ." When Ranko telephoned the apartment from the dressing room, her husband answered in a sleepy voice.

"Is that so? I'll draw up the string, then."

"No, don't do that. I've got a good idea." Ranko smiled into the mouthpiece. "They're nothing but rowdy little shop boys, but they call out my name when I'm onstage. They're important publicity agents for me. I'm thinking I'd like to thank them in a clever way. Something to eat—bean-jam buns would be good. Please tie some onto the string. They probably haven't had anything to eat since this morning. They'll be overjoyed. They'll say what a clever lady I am. I'll be more popular than ever."

"Uh-huh." Although he agreed, mingling a yawn with his assent, the poverty-stricken poet did not even have enough money to buy bean-jam buns. When he looked around the room, there was nothing except a flower wreath that Ranko had brought back from the theater.

Well, now, had the gallantry of taking pleasure in flowers rather than bread entirely died out among juvenile delinquents?

When, snickering mischievously, the boys gave the string a good hard tug, unexpectedly there was no resistance. A newspaper-wrapped parcel came rustling down. What's this? They looked up, but the third-floor window was closed. When they opened the parcel, there were flowers, flowers, and more flowers. They were the artificial flowers that Ranko's husband had plucked out of the wreath. The youths let out a cheer.

"Hey, what a clever lady!"

"A magnificent performance! We really look up to her!"

"Let's throw these flowers on the stage when Ranko's dancing tomorrow night!"

Each of them sticking a flower into the sash of his kimono, their sleeves filled with flowers, they went off.

"Hey, you guys—maybe it wasn't Ranko who did this."

"That's right. She's probably still back at the theater."

"Her husband must have done it."

"Isn't that even better?"

"Because he's a poet!"

The next night, they threw those flowers down onto the stage when Ranko danced.

However, since Ranko was a female performer of Asakusa, it wasn't only because of night rehearsals that she got back late. With her fellow performers, she often went to a noodle shop in the Yoshiwara red-light district where you could drink until three in the morning. She would also be invited by customers to the all-night actors' green room in the park. The band of shop boys saw that. Since the gift of flowers, they'd become the allies of Ranko's husband.

"Let's teach Ranko a lesson. Some of us will take her husband for a walk. While he's out, somebody will go up to the apartment and make a bundle of Ranko's clothes and makeup things and tie it to a string. When Ranko gets back all drunk and pulls on it, the bundle will come tumbling down. She'll get the message. 'Wife, get out!' That's the plan."

The night when all the arrangements had been skillfully completed, one of the shop boys jumped out at Ranko as she was being taken somewhere by a customer.

"Aren't you afraid of being kicked out by your husband if you play around like this?"

"I beg your pardon, but I've got my husband on a string."

LD

Sleeping Habit

[1932]

Startled by a sharp pain, as if her hair were being pulled out, she woke up three or four times. But when she realized that a skein of her black hair was wound around the neck of her lover, she smiled to herself. In the morning, she would say, "My hair is this long now. When we sleep together, it truly grows longer."

Quietly, she closed her eyes.

"I don't want to sleep. Why do we have to sleep? Even though we are lovers, to have to go to sleep, of all things!" On nights when it was all right for her to stay with him, she would say this, as if it were a mystery to her.

"You'd have to say that people make love precisely because they have to sleep. A love that never sleeps—the very idea is frightening. It's something thought up by a demon."

"That's not true. At first, we neither slept either, did we? There's nothing so selfish as sleep."

That was the truth. As soon as he fell asleep, he would pull his arm out from under her neck, frowning unconsciously as he did so. She, too, no matter where she embraced him, would find when she awakened that the strength had gone out of her arm.

"Well, then, I'll wind my hair around and around your arm and hold you tight."

Winding the sleeve of his sleeping kimono around her arm, she'd held him hard. Just the same, sleep stole away the strength from her fingers.

"All right, then, just as the old proverb says, I'll tie you up with the rope of a woman's hair." So saying, she'd drawn a long skein of her raven-black hair around his neck.

That morning, however, he smiled at what she said.

"What do you mean, your hair has grown longer? It's so tangled up you can't pass a comb through it."

As time went by, they forgot about that sort of thing. These nights, she slept as if she'd even forgotten he was there. But, if she happened to wake up, her arm was always touching him—and his arm was touching her. By now, when they no longer thought about it, it had become their sleeping habit.

LD

Umbrella

[1932]

The spring rain was not enough to make things wet. It was almost as light as fog, just enough to moisten the skin slightly. The girl ran outside and saw the boy's umbrella. "Oh, is it raining?"

As he passed before the shop, the boy had opened his umbrella—more to hide his shyness than to protect himself from the rain.

Even so, he silently held the umbrella out toward the girl. She put only one shoulder under it. The boy was now getting wet, but he could not bring himself to move closer to the girl to ask if she would get under it with him. Although the girl wanted to put her hand on the handle of the umbrella with the boy's, she looked as though she were about to run away.

The two went to a photographer's studio. The boy's father was to be transferred in his civil service job. This would be their parting photograph.

"Would you sit here together, please?" The photographer pointed toward the sofa, but the boy could not sit down beside the girl. He stood behind her, touching her cloak lightly with the hand he rested on the back of the sofa, wanting to feel their bodies were somehow connected. It was the first time he had ever touched her. The body heat he could perceive through his fingertips made him sense the warmth he might feel if he were to embrace her naked.

Throughout his life he would recall the warmth of her body whenever he looked at this picture.

"Would you like me to take one more? I could take a closer photograph of you side by side."

The boy simply nodded.

"What about your hair?" the boy whispered to the girl.

She looked up at the boy and blushed. Her eyes glowed with a bright joy. Meekly she scurried to the restroom.

When she had seen the boy pass by the shop earlier, she had jumped up without taking time to fix her hair. Now she was worried because her hair was disheveled as though she had just removed a bathing cap. The girl was so shy she could not even begin to do up her stray locks correctly in front of a man, but the boy had thought it would have made her more embarrassed if he had told her to fix her hair again.

The girl's cheerfulness as she ran to the restroom lightened the boy's spirits as well. When she returned, they sat next to each other on the sofa as though it were the most natural thing in the world.

As they were about to leave the studio, the boy looked around for his umbrella. Then he noticed that the girl had stepped outside ahead of him and was holding it. When she noticed the boy was watching, it suddenly occurred to her that she had taken his umbrella. The thought startled her. Had her inadvertent action shown the boy that she felt that she, too, belonged to him?

The boy could not offer to hold the umbrella, and the girl could not bring herself to hand it to him. Somehow the road now was different from the one that had brought them to the photographer's. The two had suddenly become adults. They returned home feeling as though they were a married couple—if only over this incident with the umbrella.

JMH

Death Mask

[1932]

He did not know how many lovers she had had before him. But, anyway, it was obvious that he would be her last because her death was already approaching.

"Had I known I would die this soon, I would have wished to have been killed back then." She smiled brightly. Even as he held her, the look in her eyes made it seem as though she were recalling the many men she had known.

Even when the end was about to come, she could not forget her own beauty, nor could she forget her many loves. She did not realize that this now served to make her look pained.

"The men all wanted to kill me. Though they didn't say so, in their hearts they wanted to."

The man who now held her in his arms as she was about to die harbored no anxiety that he would lose her to another, so perhaps he was fortunate compared to her previous lovers who had been tormented, knowing that there was no way to keep her heart except to kill her. But he grew tired holding her. The woman had always pursued intense love. Even after she fell ill, she could not sleep peacefully unless she could feel a man's arms around her neck or on her breast.

Gradually her condition grew worse.

"Hold my feet. My feet are so lonely I can't stand it."

Her feet felt lonely, as if death were creeping up from her toes. He sat at the foot of her bed and held her feet tightly. They were cold like death. Then, unexpectedly, his hands trembled queerly. He could perceive the vital woman through her small feet. Those small, cold feet transmitted the same joy to the man's palms that he had felt as he touched the soles of her feet when they were warm and sweaty. He felt ashamed of this sensation that sullied the sacredness of her death. But, wondering if her request that he should hold her feet might have been a last resort to the wiles of love, he grew fearful of her wretched femininity.

"You're thinking that there is something missing in our love now that there is no longer any need for jealousy. But when I die, the object of your jealousy will appear. Surely, from somewhere." She spoke, then breathed her last.

It was as she said.

An actor in the new theater came to the wake and applied makeup to the face of the dead woman as if to resurrect, once more, the fresh, vital beauty the woman had possessed when she was in love with him.

Later an artist came to spread plaster on her face. The makeup that the actor had applied earlier made the woman's face appear so alive that it looked as though the artist were smothering the woman to death out of jealousy toward the actor. The artist made the death mask in order to remember the woman's face.

Seeing that the battle of love that surrounded the woman did not end with her death, the man realized that even having her die in his arms was nothing but an empty, fleeting victory. He pondered this as he went to the artist's place to take the death mask from him.

But the death mask looked like a woman and also like a man. It looked like a young girl and also like an old woman. The man's voice sounded as though the fire in his breast had faded. "This is her, but it is not her. First of all, I can't tell if it's a man or a woman."

"That's right." The artist spoke, his face melancholy. "If

you look at a death mask not knowing who it is, you generally can't tell the sex. For example, even with a powerful face like Beethoven's, if you stare at his death mask, it begins to look like a woman's face. . . . Still, I thought her death mask would be feminine since there was no woman more womanly than she. But it is just like all the others—she couldn't beat death. The distinction of sex ends with death.

"Her whole life was the tragic drama of the joy of being a woman. Until the last moment, she was all too much a woman." He put out his hand, feeling as if a nightmare had vanished. "If she has finally escaped that tragedy, then we can shake hands now—here before this death mask in which we cannot distinguish female from male."

JMH

Faces

[1932]

From the age of six or seven until she was fourteen or fifteen, she did nothing but cry onstage. Back then, the audience would often cry, too.

The idea that the audience would always cry if she cried was the first view she had of her own life. To her, people's faces all looked as if they would cry if they saw her onstage. Since there was not a single face that she did not understand, the world to her seemed to be a readily comprehensible face.

There was not an actor in the whole company who could make so many in an audience cry the way this child actress could.

Anyway, at the age of sixteen, she gave birth to a child.

"It doesn't look a thing like me. It's not my child. I'll have nothing to do with it," the child's father said.

"It doesn't look at all like me, either," the young woman said. "But it is my child."

Her daughter's face was the first she could not understand. You might say that her life as a child actress was ruined when she gave birth to this girl, for then she realized that there was a great moat between the stage at the theater, where she cried and made the audience cry, and the world of reality. When she looked into that moat, she saw that it was pitch-black. Countless incomprehensible faces, like that of her own child, appeared in the darkness.

She left the child's father somewhere on the road.

Then, as the years passed, she began to think that the child's face resembled that of the man she had left.

Eventually, her daughter's performances began to make audiences cry, just as her own had done when she was young.

She parted with her child, too, somewhere on the road.

Later, she began to think that her daughter's face resembled her own.

Over ten years later, the young woman finally came upon her own father, an itinerant actor, at a country theater. There she learned of her mother's whereabouts.

She went to her mother. As soon as she took one look, she cried out. Sobbing, she clung to her mother. The woman saw her own mother for the first time in her life. And, for the first time ever, she truly cried.

The face of the daughter she had left on the road was an exact replica of her own mother's face. Just as the woman had not looked like her own mother, she and her own child had not looked alike. But grandmother and granddaughter were precise duplicates of each other.

As the woman cried on her mother's breast, she realized that she *had* truly been crying when she was a child actress.

Now, her heart like that of a pilgrim to a holy land, the woman went back to the groups of itinerant performers to find her daughter and the girl's father and tell them about the faces.

JMH

The Younger Sister's Clothes

[1932]

Lately, the older sister had often worn the clothes of her younger sister. She often took evening walks in the park where the younger sister had walked with her fiancé.

Evenings in the park, from spring into autumn, tens and hundreds of couples walked hand in hand. It was a park with few lamps and many shadowy trees.

Their house was in back of the park.

Telling her to walk her fiancé as far as the trolley stop in front of the park, the older sister had often sent the younger sister out of the house.

Nowadays, however, the older sister often went to the doctor's house in the neighborhood in front of the park to get her sister's medicine.

Her sister's clothes, which she herself wore now, had all been bought by her for her sister's marriage.

"You only buy clothes for me that are more conservative than your own," her sister had frequently complained.

"I don't want you to spend your life dressed up in flashy, crazy clothes like I do. That's why I'm going to all this trouble."

"I should work without having any fun—isn't that what you're saying?"

"Even you should be able to tell what kind of life it is when there's no difference between going-out and staying-at-home clothes."

"It would be better than doing nothing, like this."

Changing jobs at a dizzying rate, from geisha to movie actress to taxi dancer, the older sister was currently a "new-dance" performer at a small revue theater in Asakusa. She'd gotten the young manager of the theater to buy her a house, so she could afford to appear onstage only when she felt like it. Shortly after becoming a movie actress, she had summoned her younger sister from the country. She had wanted to give to the younger sister what for her already seemed impossible—the greatest blessing in this life, a beautiful marriage.

The older sister had selected a husband for the younger sister, and she had prepared the younger sister's trousseau. She saw her dream self in the girl. How hard she had worked, these two or three years—as though she were working for nothing else—for the wedding of this younger sister who by now was her second self.

"My sister knows absolutely nothing about the world. It's as if she had never seen anyone but myself." As she smiled at the younger sister's fiancé, the tears almost came. She felt drunk with the pleasure of being able to say such a thing.

Like the design of the clothes she had bought for her sister, the husband she had chosen for her was an ordinary man.

Her sister, who had never been exposed to the winds of the world, would never know what pains she had taken for her, the older sister thought. She was surprised by her sister's fearless manner of speech with the man. Although perfectly polite, it was far more audacious than her own rough way of talking. With her own man, the sister had grown more and more derisive, continually finding fault.

Ever since the marriage, the younger sister had frequently complained about the inadequacy of her commonplace husband.

"You're fortunate to be able to come out and say such self-indulgent things, to me of all people." Her head bowed, the older sister bit her lip.

When she fell ill, the younger sister immediately returned to the older sister's house. She seemed to take pleasure in her illness as a pretext for divorce. But her spinal disease promised an early death. The younger sister did not know that. The older sister, who did know, came to feel as if her sister were her own child.

"This child is mine and mine alone."

Her sister was encased in a corset under her kimono that, like a fencer's armor, held her upright. It had round holes carved out for the breasts and made her look as if she were with child. As the autumn deepened, her hands became cold to the touch. In her gaunt face, her cheeks glowed a hectic red, her eyes grew large and moist. When she put on makeup that was even heavier than her sister's, she possessed a sort of beautiful dirtiness.

Eventually, the corset was set out to air in a sunny spot on the veranda. Then, when the younger sister took to her bed, the corset was discarded in a corner of the garden. The younger sister became unable to leave her bed. When it snowed, the corset turned white with the rest of the garden. In the two windows carved out in its chest, those round little windows where her sister's breasts had peeped out, sparrows perched, their heads flicking from side to side in a perfect snowy morning scene. It was like a painful fairy tale.

The older sister thought she would like to have the husband up, to show him how things were. She wanted to tell him that a death like her sister's, in which the strength to live imperceptibly ebbed away, was merciful, that it lacked any real grief.

The younger sister's husband, after his wife had become unable to leave her bed, slept at the older sister's house and went to the office from there. Although the sister, in her sickbed, reverted to the feelings of a child, she began to yearn for her husband and her husband only. In the older sister's eyes, this change seemed pitiful, for now both her sister and the husband seemed to have forgotten death in their love for each other.

The younger sister, like an imbecile tyrant, would not let her husband leave her bedside.

"I don't like it when you go to the bathhouse," she would say, or, "I don't like it when you read the newspaper." She was absolutely unable to bear the loneliness of lying awake alone in the dead of night. Tying her husband's hand and her own with a narrow red sash, she would pull on it and get her husband out of bed any number of times.

"You've really been very good to her." Before going on, the older sister made sure that what she was feeling was not jealousy. "It's sad to say, but in a little while it will all be over."

When he came back from the office, the younger sister's husband often stood rooted to the ground in the earthen entryway where the older sister had come out to greet him. The sister's heart was also full. Neither said a word. To the husband, the older sister seemed to have become the younger sister.

After the younger sister had returned to the older sister's house and taken to her bed, the older sister had frequently worn the younger sister's clothes.

Nowadays, the older sister made do with just three or four changes of seasonal best clothes. The clothes that she had bought two or three years ago for her sister's trousseau were too conservative for her even as she was now. She looked so young and resembled her sister so much that one would have taken them to be the same age. Her sister, as she wasted away, no longer seemed like a human being but rather like a withered flower or that snow-covered corset in the garden. The older sister resembled neither her sister as she was now nor as she had been before her illness: She resembled both. Sitting at the mirror, she had often discovered her younger sister in it. Not only was she wearing her sister's clothes, but, without realizing it, she had begun to do up her hair in the same way her sister once had done.

So, at night, it was now the older sister who went through the park, where her sister had strolled with her fiancé, to get medicine for her. Although vaguely aware that she had come to resemble her sister more and more, she kept going that way.

One night near spring, when the pairs of lovers had begun to appear in the park, the older sister, again wearing her sister's clothes, hurried along the path. She was on her way to inform the doctor that her sister's death from complications of peritonitis seemed only a few hours away. It was evidently closing hour at the library in the park. She remembered having cut through a crowd of people outside but did not notice that someone was following her.

"Kotoko." Suddenly called by her sister's name, she turned around.

"Ah, so it was Kotoko after all." A man whom she'd never seen before came up alongside her.

"You're mistaken. Kotoko . . ."

"Are you saying that you know what your name is but that I've forgotten it?"

"Kotoko's at home. She's dying."

Both the older sister and the stranger were breathing fast.

"That again? You said before that I was to think that Kotoko had died. You said that out of duty to your sister or somebody, you were getting married, the same as if you were dying."

Astonished at first, the older sister became calm. Had her sister also had a lover? She tried to make out the man's face, close to hers in the dark night.

How strange, on the night of her sister's death, to be mistaken for her by her sister's lover.

"Telling me that I should think of you as dead, when . . ." The man gripped the older sister's shoulder. "When you're alive like this." He shook her roughly. The older sister staggered.

"Forgive me," she inadvertently muttered. She meant it as an apology to her sister. Concealing the fact that she had a lover, her sister had married the man she had chosen for her. She had made herself into the older sister's puppet. The strength went out of the older sister's body. She forgot the man's arms around her.

The man held the woman, who seemed to be collapsing, against his chest.

Did her sister's lover still love her sister? Changing into her sister, she knew the man's heart. The thought came to her that she should tell her dying sister about this. Unexpectedly, her tears overflowed.

"You still love me. You love me this much." The man, supporting the older sister, led her under the shadow of a tree.

In the man's arms, the older sister vividly imagined her dying sister, held like this in her husband's arms. As she did the man's will, she saw herself marrying her sister's husband after her sister's death. The vision set up a wild storm in her blood.

The older sister, who had sought in her younger sister what she herself had lost, had recovered it for herself by her sister's death.

LD

The Wife of the Autumn Wind

[1933]

He'd seen the woman off. The hotel corridors and entryway were as quiet as a mirror in which were reflected the pale, fleeting clouds of autumn. Somehow he didn't feel right about simply going back to his room on the second floor. Pausing on the landing, he picked out the book the farthest to the right on the bookshelf. With the book, a cricket almost leapt out at him. The book was an encyclopedia. On the page he opened to was this entry: "The Wife of the Autumn Wind. Edo Period comic *tanka* poet. Niece of Daimojiya-fumiro of the Yoshiwara, wife of Kabocha Motonari. So called from her authorship of the poem: 'The wind noises abroad Autumn's coming / And breaks the seal of the seventh month / Scattering a single paulownia leaf.' Also wrote many *waka*."

"What trivial stuff." He didn't really understand the poem. When you are on a boring trip, you pick up all sorts of tidbits of unnecessary information, he thought. He continued upstairs. In his room there was the smell of cosmetics. In the wastepaper basket beside the dressing table, there were many little coils of hair.

"Well, have this many come out? How sad." He gathered them up from the basket. Probably the lady, surprised at her loss of hair, had wound them around her finger as she looked at them. The hairs were curled up in tight circles.

He went out onto the veranda. The automobile in which the woman was riding ran along the straight white highway. He'd shut his right eye and placed a circlet of hair against his left, narrowing the eye as if looking through a lens; through this, he followed the distant car. It seemed like a metal flower or toy. Somehow he felt as pleased as a child. But the hair had a musty scent, as if the woman hadn't washed her hair in a long time. It smelled of hardship. It was already that time of year when, if he'd cradled the woman's head, he might have been startled by the coldness of her hair.

Their relationship was such that he'd merely lent her his room for half an hour. Suffering from tuberculosis, the woman's husband had come to this hotel for a change of climate. Priding himself on the strength of his spirit, insisting that he could overcome his sickness by force of faith, he would not let her leave his side for a minute. However, death was already only two or three days away. The wife had to return to their house in Tokyo to make preparations; probably it concerned money or other such irksome matters. Coming secretly to his room, where she'd left a change of clothes, she had dressed for her journey and stolen out of the hotel.

The woman, always wearing a white coverall, had come and gone in the corridors of the hotel with a melancholy face. In this fashionable place, bustling with foreign visitors summer and winter, her drab figure had gone straight to his heart with its homely beauty. Truly she was "the wife of the autumn wind."

The automobile was hidden by the tip of the promontory.

"Mommy, Mommy!" Calling out in a crystal-clear voice, an English boy of four or five bounded out onto the lawn. Behind him came the mother, accompanied by two Pekingese dogs. The transparent sweetness of the child made him think that the old Western paintings of angels were not mere fabrications. The withered lawn, although some green remained in its depths, reminded him of the silence of a convent from which the nuns have departed. The boy and the dogs scampered off into the pine forest. Above the forest there should have been a straight dark blue ribbon of sea; in the two or three years since his last visit, had the tops of the pines reached up to hide it? From the direction of that invisible sea, the sky was clouding up with fearful rapidity.

About to go back into his room, he heard dance music. It was teatime, but not a single guest had come down to tea. The lights were already on in the hall. Through the plate-glass window, he could see the head clerk and a woman who looked like a senior chambermaid, the only couple on the floor, dancing to the strains of a waltz. The plump chambermaid had on a Western dress that fit her badly around the hips. She seemed to be a very poor dancer.

Coming in from the veranda, he lay down with his head on his elbow and went to sleep. When he woke up, there was the sound of dead leaves scurrying over the ground in the garden in back of the inn. The glass doors rattled. The sounds were harbingers of an autumn typhoon.

"I wonder how that sick man is. Has his wife come back yet?" He felt uneasy. About to telephone the desk, he felt, somehow, eyes looking at him from the depths of autumn. Abruptly, rebelliously, he felt a powerful, possessive love for the woman.

LD

A Pet Dog's Safe Birthing

[1935]

Since old times, Iwata obis have been worn on the dog days of summer because a dog's labor when she is giving birth is as light as an Iwata obi. I have acted as a midwife for a dog many times. The birth of new life is a good thing, and breeding and raising dogs is a great joy for those who keep them. But last year I had a hard time with two difficult births one after the other.

It was the wirehaired terrier's first time. The terrier's third puppy suffocated in the birth canal, and the veterinarian had to pull the fourth one out with forceps. But the first two puppies and the mother lived.

The collie was a bigger problem. She had passed her due date by a week, then ten days, without giving birth. That is quite rare in dogs. I could not sleep, wondering if it would be that night. I called two veterinarians and even had a friend of mine who was an obstetrician for humans come over.

The three of them argued and argued about whether or not they should operate to determine if the puppies were alive or dead. Finally they performed a cesarean section. The mother's prognosis had looked favorable, but she died that night. The seven puppies inside her had been half-rotten.

I calculated the loss in money resulting from these two difficult births to be over a thousand yen. That aside, after the collie died it seemed so lonely that I moved from my house in Sakuragi-chō. The collie's behavior had been that of a spoiled child. She would never leave my side when I stayed up through the night writing. She would rub her head on my lap. Even when I went to the bathroom, she would follow me. The experience with her made me realize the uncertainty of veterinary obstetrics as compared with the remarkable advances in human obstetrics. When an important dog is having a difficult birth, it would be good to have an obstetrician for humans present.

The next birthing was the terrier's second. Seeing her scratching around in the straw in her box at about eleven o'clock at night, I knew she was about to give birth. I gave her plenty of egg yolk and oatmeal and arranged all the maternity equipment: absorbent cotton, scissors, a length of fine samisen string, alcohol, and such. The dog's box was placed beside the desk where I work. Just for that night, my wife, still dressed in her kimono, slept under the *kotatsu** behind me. This dog lived to follow my wife around, so the dog could not be calmed, even for a moment, unless she could see my wife.

At last, the dog brazenly left the box and went to my wife's pillow. She walked around and around on the quilt near my wife's shoulder, as though she were going to give birth right there. My wife was sleeping, unaware. Finally, the dog's breathing became heavy. She yawned and made a strange face as if to say, "Why does my stomach hurt so much when I'm tired?" Moaning, she turned in circles. As I waited, I read Niwa Fumio's first story, "Sweetwater Trout."

Shortly after three in the morning, real labor finally began. I checked the birth canal. The time was right, so I moved her to the box. While she was looking up at me, straining, her water broke, and she licked the bottom of the box. When I finally peeped in, a puppy was being born. It was about four o'clock.

*A low table with a wide quilted skirt and a heating element underneath.

"Hey! They're coming. She's having her puppies. Wake up! They're being born."

My wife jumped up, but, when she saw the blood, her hands trembled and she got flustered. The puppy was in a sac that looked like a stuffed intestine or a balloon. I was used to it.

Of course, the mother dog first licked the placenta and tried to bite it and pull it away. The puppy looked like a drowned rat, but in a moment it opened its mouth and started moving. I cut the umbilical cord with the scissors; I had planned to tie it with string first, then cut the cord, but it was too much trouble, so I just cut it as it was. Actually, I cut the placenta first, then cut the umbilical cord. I must not mistake the order.

I wrapped the placenta in absorbent cotton and took it out. The mother dog would be expected to eat it, but there is a theory that it is not good for the dog's stomach to eat the placenta, and there is also a theory that it makes the milk come in well if she does. Since there is one piece of placenta for each puppy, I thought it best to give her one or two..

The puppy became much more lively and began to crawl more the longer I watched, as if some mysterious life force were flowing into it from its mother's tongue as she licked it. The puppy looked for its mother's milk. I wiped both the puppy and its mother with cotton.

"Well, this one is living, anyway. It has a good pattern on its coat, but it's a bit small." I felt relieved. I wiped the blood from my hands as my wife leaned over the box.

"It's better if they're small. This birthing is easier than last time with the bigger ones. Won't there be a lot more of them in there? It's somehow frightening. I can't touch the puppy. Is it going to find the milk?"

I picked up the puppy and looked at its underside. It was a female.

The second puppy came a little later, about four-forty. It was stuck in the birth canal for a bit. It was a male, larger than the first puppy. It was lively, and its whitish head made it look quite innocent. My wife put the wet puppy inside her kimono to warm it against her skin. She wiped it with cotton.

"I'm glad two are living—the same as last time," she said to the dog to comfort her. Less than ten minutes later, the third puppy slid out. It was a male with a black mask. I gave the placenta to the mother. I wiped the puppy dry, but he crawled to the back once more and got wet again, his head covered with blood. My wife then put him in her kimono and warmed him. She had forgotten her initial fear.

"Ugh! They cling to my breast. It hurts."

The mother dog still trusted my wife absolutely, but she looked left and right as though thinking it strange that her babies' cries should come from inside my wife's kimono.

Then, from the other side of the room, something called. It was my pet horned owl. The scene of the birth and the puppies' cries were all so bizarre, the owl could hardly contain himself. He not only cocked his head and stretched to see, but he also went around in circles, staring at the box.

"Oh, are you here, too? I forgot all about you." I stood up and fed him a bagworm.

The fourth puppy—of course, a male—was born about five-twenty. My wife said there would be more, but about six o'clock I stood the mother dog up and checked her. Her belly seemed empty. It was all too easy a delivery. The mother gobbled up the egg yolk and oatmeal and drank some water. The puppies' paws and mouths were a pure blood color, the color of robust youth. There were also faint black spots on their noses. Having fulfilled my duty, I wiped my sticky hands, read the morning paper, and thought about traveling.

My wife kept saying, "Good, oh, good. Babies certainly sleep a lot." She rubbed the mother dog's sides.

I counted the names of my old friends, Ishihama Kinsaku, Suzuki Hikojirō, Suga Tadao, Ozaki Shirō, and Takeda Rintarō, who all had babies that my wife had not yet seen, and I told her we would go visit them all. I got up to change the bedding. When I opened the shutters, the warm morning filled the room with light.

January 18

JMH

Hometown

[1944]

When Kinuko returned to visit her parents' home, she recalled the time when her sister-in-law had gone back to visit her own hometown.

In her sister-in-law's mountain village, there was a tradition called the "dumpling feast." Every year on the evening of January thirty-first all the girls who had married and moved away were invited back to the village to eat dumplings in bean soup.

"You still want to go, even in all this snow?" Kinuko's mother had asked a bit crossly as she had watched her daughter-in-law put her baby on her back and leave. "Can she really enjoy it that much? She has children of her own, and there she is acting like a child herself. Why, if she doesn't develop some kind of feeling for this home . . ."

Then Kinuko had said, "But if I were to go away somewhere, Mother, this home would always be dear to me. And if I didn't look forward to coming home, you would miss me, wouldn't you, Mother?"

The village was short of men because of the war. The daughter-in-law was such a hard worker that she had gone to work in the fields. Kinuko, who had gone to the city to marry, had had a rather easy life, and she felt that something was missing. Now, as she recalled the memory of her sister-in-law trudging over the mountain pass to return to her hometown in the blinding snow, a shout of encouragement almost rose in Kinuko's throat.

Four years later, after marrying and moving away, Kinuko herself returned to visit her home. She awoke to the sound of her sister-in-law in the kitchen. The mountains pressed in close on the white wall next door. The memory came back to her. Silent tears welled up in her eyes as she spoke to her late father before the family altar. "I am happy."

She went to wake her husband.

"So here we are, back in your old house!" Her husband looked about the parlor.

Since before breakfast, Kinuko's mother had been peeling piles of apples and pears. She pushed some toward her reluctant son-in-law. "Here, eat up and remember when you were young." She scolded her grandchildren, who were clamoring for some of the fruit. Kinuko delighted in her husband's gentleness, as he was besieged by his nieces and nephews.

Kinuko's mother carried the baby outside. "Look how big Kinuko's baby has grown," she bragged to someone standing nearby.

Kinuko's sister-in-law went to show her husband's letter from the front to her mother-in-law. As Kinuko watched her from behind, she perceived her sister-in-law's age—and the weight that had settled on her when she had become a member of this family. Kinuko was startled.

JMH

Water

[1944]

As soon as the woman arrived from the homeland to marry the man, he was transferred to a meteorological observation station in the Hsing-an mountain range in Manchuria. What surprised the woman most was that it cost seven sen for one oilcan full of water—cloudy, dirty water. She felt queasy just thinking that she was to use this water to rinse her mouth or wash rice. Within six months, the sheets and underwear had all turned yellow. And, to top it all off, in December the well froze solid all the way to the bottom. A coolie brought a block of ice from somewhere, and she used it occasionally for a bath. This was no place to talk of extravagance. What a blessing it would be to warm her benumbed bones! She recalled the bath in her home village as if it were a distant dream: Her arms and legs were beautiful as she held a white towel and lowered herself into the hot water up to her shoulders.

"Excuse me, but if you have any water left, could I have a little?" A neighbor woman came over, carrying an earthenware bottle. "I was polishing my pans for the first time in a long while, and forgot and used all of mine."

There was no water left, but she gave the neighbor some leftover tea.

"I can't wait until spring when I can slosh my laundry around as much as I like. How good it would feel if I could just splash some water," the neighbor woman said. This was the wish of a woman from the Japan homeland, where pure water was abundant. She could hardly wait for the runoff from the melting snow. It would be pleasant to see the water sucked into the soil when she poured it out of the basin. Dandelions would be the first thing to push up buds through that soil.

She invited the neighbor woman to take a bath in her bath-water. Then suddenly the train headed for the northern boundary came up through the valley. It was time for news concerning conditions on the southern battlefront.

"It's so vast," the neighbor woman said from the warm bathtub. Indeed, from the meteorological station far north where the woman's husband worked, all the way down to the skies of the South Seas. That is the Japan of today.

When the woman stepped out in front of her house, the frost flowers that had been formed by the fog on the tiny twigs of the larch trees were falling all about like cherry blossoms. When she lifted her eyes, the perfectly blue sky made her think of the seas of her homeland.

JMH

The Silver Fifty-Sen Pieces

[1946]

It was a custom that the two-yen allowance that she received at the start of each month, in silver fifty-sen pieces, be placed in Yoshiko's purse by her mother's own hand.

At that time, the fifty-sen piece had recently been reduced in size. These silver coins, which looked light and felt heavy, seemed to Yoshiko to fill up her small red leather purse with a solid dignity. Often, careful not to waste them, she kept them in her handbag until the end of the month. It was not that Yoshiko spurned such girlish pleasures as going out to a movie theater or a coffee shop with the friends she worked with; she simply saw those diversions as being outside her life. She had never experienced them, and so was never tempted by them.

Once a week, on her way back from the office, she would stop off at a department store and buy, for ten sen, a loaf of the seasoned French bread she liked so much. Other than that, there was nothing she particularly wanted for herself.

One day, however, at Mitsukoshi's, in the stationery department, a glass paperweight caught her eye. Hexagonal, it had a dog carved on it in relief. Charmed by the dog, Yoshiko took the paperweight in her hand. Its thrilling coolness, its unexpected weightiness, suddenly gave her pleasure. Yoshiko, who loved this kind of delicately accomplished work, was captivated despite herself. Weighing it in her palm, looking at it from every angle, she quietly and reluctantly put it back in its box. It was forty sen.

The next day, she came back. She examined the paperweight again. The day after that, she came back again and examined it anew. After ten days of this, she finally made up her mind.

"I'll take this," she said to the clerk, her heart beating fast.

When she got home, her mother and older sister laughed at her.

"Buying this sort of thing—it's like a toy."

But when each had taken it in her hand and looked at it, they said, "You're right, it *is* rather pretty," and, "It's so ingenious."

They tried holding it up against the light. The polished clear glass surface and the misty surface, like frosted glass, of the relief, harmonized curiously. In the hexagonal facets, too, there was an exquisite rightness, like the meter of a poem. To Yoshiko, it was a lovely work of art.

Although Yoshiko hadn't hoped to be complimented on the deliberation with which she had made her purchase, taking ten days to decide that the paperweight was an object worth her possession, she was pleased to receive this recognition of her good taste from her mother and older sister.

Even if she was laughed at for her exaggerated carefulness—taking those ten days to buy something that cost a mere forty sen—Yoshiko would not have been satisfied unless she had done so. She had never had occasion to regret having bought something on the spur of the moment. It was not that the seventeen-year-old Yoshiko possessed such meticulous discrimination that she spent several days thinking about and looking at something before arriving at a decision. It was just that she had a vague dread of spending carelessly the silver fifty-sen pieces, which had sunk into her mind as an important treasure.

Years later, when the story of the paperweight came up and everybody burst out laughing, her mother said seriously, "I thought you were so lovable that time."

To each and every one of Yoshiko's possessions, an amusing anecdote of this sort was attached.

It was a pleasure to do their shopping from the top down, descending regularly from floor to floor, so first they went up to the fifth floor on the elevator. This Sunday, unusually allured by the charm of a shopping trip with her mother, Yoshiko had come to Mitsukoshi's.

Although their shopping for the day was done, when they'd descended to the first floor, her mother, as a matter of course, went on down to the bargain basement.

"But it's so crowded, Mother. I don't like it," grumbled Yoshiko, but her mother didn't hear her. Evidently the atmosphere of the bargain basement, with its competitive jockeying for position, had already absorbed her mother.

The bargain basement was a place set up for the sole purpose of making people waste their money, but perhaps her mother would find something. Thinking she'd keep an eye on her, Yoshiko followed her at a distance. It was air-conditioned so it wasn't all that hot.

First buying three bundles of stationery for twenty-five sen, her mother turned around and looked at Yoshiko. They smiled sweetly at each other. Lately, her mother had been pilfering Yoshiko's stationery, much to the latter's annoyance. Now we can rest easy, their looks seemed to say.

Drawn toward the counters for kitchen utensils and underwear, Yoshiko's mother was not brave enough to thrust her way through the mob of customers. Standing on tiptoe and peering over people's shoulders or putting her hand out through the small spaces between their sleeves, she looked but nevertheless didn't buy anything. At first unconvinced and then making up her mind definitely no, she headed toward the exit.

"Oh, these are just ninety-five sen? My . . ."

Just this side of the exit, her mother picked up one of the umbrellas for sale. Even after they'd burrowed through the whole heaped-up jumble, every single umbrella bore a price tag of ninety-five sen.

Apparently still surprised, her mother said, "They're so cheap, aren't they, Yoshiko? Aren't they cheap?" Her voice was suddenly lively. It was as if her vague, perplexed reluctance to leave without buying something more had found an outlet. "Well? Don't you think they're cheap?"

"They really are." Yoshiko, too, took one of the umbrellas in her hand. Her mother, holding hers alongside it, opened it up.

"Just the ribs alone would be cheap at the price. The fabric—well, it's rayon, but it's so well made, don't you think?"

How was it possible to sell such a respectable item at this price? As the question flashed through Yoshiko's mind, a strange feeling of antipathy welled up in her, as if she'd been shoved by a cripple. Her mother, totally absorbed, opening up one after the other, rummaged through the pile to find an umbrella suitable to her age. Yoshiko waited a while, then said, "Mother, don't you have an umbrella at home?"

"Yes, that's so, but . . ." Glancing quickly at Yoshiko, her mother went on, "It's ten years, no, more, I've had it fifteen years. It's worn-out and old-fashioned. And, Yoshiko, if I passed this on to somebody, think how happy they would be."

"That's true. It's all right if it's for a gift."

"There's nobody who wouldn't be happy."

Yoshiko smiled. Her mother seemed to be choosing an umbrella with that "somebody" in mind. But it was not anybody close to them. If it were, surely her mother would not have said "somebody."

"What about this one, Yoshiko?"

"That looks good."

Although she gave an unenthusiastic answer, Yoshiko went to her mother's side and began searching for a suitable umbrella.

Other shoppers, wearing thin summer dresses of rayon and saying, "It's cheap, it's cheap," were casually snapping up the umbrellas on their way into and out of the store.

Feeling pity for her mother, who, her face set and slightly flushed, was trying so hard to find the right umbrella, Yoshiko grew angry at her own hesitation.

As if to say, "Why not just buy one, any one, quickly?" Yoshiko turned away from her mother.

"Yoshiko, let's stop this."

"What?"

A weak smile floating at the corners of her mouth, as if to shake something off, her mother put her hand on Yoshiko's shoulder and left the counter. Now, though, it was Yoshiko who felt some indefinable reluctance. But, when she'd taken five or six steps, she felt relieved.

Taking hold of her mother's hand on her shoulder, she squeezed it hard and swung it together with her own. Pressing close to her mother so that they were shoulder to shoulder, she hurried toward the exit.

This had happened seven years ago, in the year 1939.

When the rain pounded against the fire-scorched sheet-metal roof of the shack, Yoshiko, thinking it would have been good if they had bought that umbrella, found herself wanting to make a funny story of it with her mother. Nowadays, the umbrella would have cost a hundred or two hundred yen. But her mother had died in the firebombings of their Tokyo neighborhood of Kanda.

Even if they had bought the umbrella, it probably would have perished in the flames.

By chance, the glass paperweight had survived. When her husband's house in Yokohama had burned down, the paperweight was among those things that she'd frantically stuffed into an emergency bag. It was her one remembrance of life in her mother's house.

From evening on, in the alley, there were the strange-sounding voices of the neighborhood girls. They were talking about how you could make a thousand yen in a single night. Taking up the forty-sen paperweight, which, when she was those girls' age, she had spent ten days thinking about before deciding to buy, Yoshiko studied the charming little dog carved in relief. Suddenly, she realized that there was not a single dog left in the whole burned-out neighborhood. The thought came as a shock to her.

LD

Tabi

[1948]

If my sister was such a gentle person, why did she have to die that way? I didn't understand.

Turning delirious in the evening, my sister arched her body back. Her braced, straining hands trembled violently. Even when that stopped, her head seemed about to drop off the pillow to the left. And then, from her half-opened mouth, a white intestinal roundworm slowly crawled out.

Since then, I've often recalled vividly the peculiar whiteness of that worm. And, at such times, I make it a point to think of the white socks called *tabi*.

When we were placing various articles in my sister's coffin, I said, "Mother, what about the *tabi*? Let's put them in, too."

"That's good. I'd forgotten about them. Because this child had pretty feet."

"Size nine. Let's be sure we don't mix hers up with yours or mine," I said.

I mentioned the *tabi* not only because my sister's feet were small and beautiful but also because of a memory of such socks.

It was in December of my twelfth year. In the nearby town, the Isami Tabi Company was sponsoring a film festival. A publicity band that went around from town to town, red streamers flying, came out to our village. Movie tickets were said to be mixed in with the fliers scattered by the band. We village children followed behind the band and picked up all the fliers. Actually, it was a trick to get us to buy the socks so we could use the labels as movie tickets. Back then, in villages like ours, except for fair days or the big Bon Festival, there was almost no chance of seeing a movie. The socks sold well.

I, too, picked up a flier, on which there was a picture of a dashing "man-about-town." Early that evening, I went into town and stood in the line outside the little movie theater. I felt uneasy and fearful. Would the flier turn out not to be a ticket?

"What is this? It's nothing but a flier." I was laughed at by the ticket-taker. Crestfallen, I went home. Somehow I could not bring myself to go into the house. Full of loneliness, I loitered by the well. My sister came out with a bucket to draw some water. Putting her hand on my shoulder, she asked me what the matter was. I covered my face with my hands. Leaving the bucket there, my sister went inside and came back out with the money.

"Go quickly now."

When I turned at the street corner and looked back, my sister was standing there, seeing me off. I ran off as fast as I could. At the sock-maker's in town, I was asked, "What size do you want?"

I was flustered.

"Take off that one you're wearing, then."

Inside the clasp, "nine" was written.

When I got back, I handed the socks to my sister. She was size nine, too.

About two years went by. Our family had moved to Korea and was living in Seoul. In the third year of girls' school, I fell in love with my teacher, Mr. Mitsuhashi. I was watched over at home and forbidden to visit him. Mr. Mitsuhashi caught a cold and developed complications, so there were no end-of-term tests.

Going out with my mother before Christmas, I thought I would buy Mr. Mitsuhashi a get-well present. I bought a scarlet satin top hat. In the ribbon of the hat, a sprig of rich dark green holly with a red cluster of berries had been inserted. Inside were chocolates wrapped in silver foil.

When I entered the bookstore on the avenue, I met my sister. I showed her my parcel.

"Guess what this is! It's a present for Mr. Mitsuhashi."

"You shouldn't have done that." My sister spoke in a low voice, as if taking me to task. "Weren't you told not to, even at school?"

My happiness evaporated. For the first time, I felt that my sister and I were completely separate persons.

The red top hat stayed on my worktable, and Christmas passed. But, on the thirtieth of that last month of the year, the top hat disappeared. Even the shadow of my happiness has disappeared, I thought. I could not even ask my sister what had happened to the hat.

The following day, New Year's Eve, my sister invited me out for a walk.

"I offered those chocolates in Mr. Mitsuhashi's memory. They were like a red jewel in the shade of the white flowers. It was pretty. I asked that they be placed in the coffin."

I hadn't known that Mr. Mitsuhashi had died. After putting the red top hat on my worktable, I hadn't gone out. Evidently everyone in the house had concealed Mr. Mitsuhashi's death from me.

So far, that red top hat and these white Japanese socks are the only things that I have ever placed in a coffin. I heard that Mr. Mitsuhashi, on his thin pallet in the cheap boardinghouse, his breath rattling in his throat, his eyeballs starting from their sockets, died in agony.

What did they mean, that red top hat and those white *tabi*? I, who am alive, ask myself.

LD

The Jay

[1949]

Since daybreak, the jay had been singing noisily.

When they'd slid open the rain shutters, it had flown up before their eyes from a lower branch of the pine, but it seemed to have come back. During breakfast, there was the sound of whirring wings.

"That bird's a nuisance." The younger brother started to get to his feet.

"It's all right. It's all right." The grandmother stopped him. "It's looking for its child. Apparently the chick fell out of the nest yesterday. It was flying around until late in the evening. Doesn't she know where it is? But what a good mother. This morning she came right back to look."

"Grandmother understands well," Yoshiko said.

Her grandmother's eyes were bad. Aside from a bout with nephritis about ten years ago, she had never been ill in her life. But, because of her cataracts, which she'd had since girlhood, she could only see dimly out of her left eye. One had to hand her the rice bowl and the chopsticks. Although she could grope her way around the familiar interior of the house, she could not go into the garden by herself.

Sometimes, standing or sitting in front of the sliding-glass door, she would spread out her hands, fanning out her fingers against the sunlight that came through the glass, and gaze out. She was concentrating all the life that was left to her into that many-angled gaze.

At such times, Yoshiko was frightened by her grandmother. Though she wanted to call out to her from behind, she would furtively steal away.

This nearly blind grandmother, simply from having heard the jay's voice, spoke as if she had seen everything. Yoshiko was filled with wonder.

When, clearing away the breakfast things, Yoshiko went into the kitchen, the jay was singing from the roof of the neighbor's house.

In the back garden, there was a chestnut tree and two or three persimmon trees. When she looked at the trees, she saw that a light rain was falling. It was the sort of rain that you could not tell was falling unless you saw it against the dense foliage.

The jay, shifting its perch to the chestnut tree, then flying low and skimming the ground, returned again to its branch, singing all the while.

The mother bird could not fly away. Was it because her chick was somewhere around there?

Worrying about it, Yoshiko went to her room. She had to get herself ready before the morning was over.

In the afternoon, her father and mother were coming with the mother of Yoshiko's fiancé.

Sitting at her mirror, Yoshiko glanced at the white stars under her fingernails. It was said that, when stars came out under your nails, it was a sign that you would receive something, but Yoshiko remembered having read in the newspaper that it meant a deficiency of vitamin C or something. The job of putting on her makeup went fairly pleasantly. Her eyebrows and lips all became unbearably winsome. Her kimono, too, went on easily.

She'd thought of waiting for her mother to come and

help with her clothes, but it was better to dress by herself, she decided.

Her father lived away from them. This was her second mother.

When her father had divorced her first mother, Yoshiko had been four and her younger brother two. The reasons given for the divorce were that her mother went around dressed in flashy clothes and spent money wildly, but Yoshiko sensed dimly that it was more than that, that the real cause lay deeper down.

Her brother, as a child, had come across a photograph of their mother and shown it to their father. The father hadn't said anything but, with a face of terrible anger, had suddenly torn the photograph to bits.

When Yoshiko was thirteen, she had welcomed the new mother to the house. Later, Yoshiko had come to think that her father had endured his loneliness for ten years for her sake. The second mother was a good person. A peaceful home life continued.

When the younger brother, entering upper school, began living away from home in a dormitory, his attitude toward his stepmother changed noticeably.

"Elder sister, I've met our mother. She's married and lives in Azabu. She's really beautiful. She was happy to see me."

Hearing this suddenly, Yoshiko could not say a word. Her face paled, and she began to tremble.

From the next room, her stepmother came in and sat down.

"It's a good thing, a good thing. It's not bad to meet your own mother. It's only natural. I've known for some time that this day would come. I don't think anything particular of it."

But the strength seemed to have gone out of her stepmother's body. To Yoshiko, her emaciated stepmother seemed pathetically frail and small.

Her brother abruptly got up and left. Yoshiko felt like smacking him.

"Yoshiko, don't say anything to him. Speaking to him will only make that boy go bad." Her stepmother spoke in a low voice.

Tears came to Yoshiko's eyes.

Her father summoned her brother back home from the dormitory. Although Yoshiko had thought that would settle the matter, her father had then gone off to live elsewhere with her stepmother.

It had frightened Yoshiko. It was as if she had been crushed by the power of masculine indignation and resentment. Did their father dislike even them because of their tie to their first mother? It seemed to her that her brother, who'd gotten to his feet so abruptly, had inherited the frightening male intransigence of his father.

And yet it also seemed to Yoshiko that she could now understand her father's sadness and pain during those ten years between his divorce and remarriage.

And so, when her father, who had moved away from her, came back bringing a marriage proposal, Yoshiko had been surprised.

"I've caused you a great deal of trouble. I told the young man's mother that you're a girl with these circumstances and that, rather than treating you like a bride, she should try to bring back the happy days of your childhood."

When her father said this kind of thing to her, Yoshiko wept.

If Yoshiko married, there would be no woman's hand to take care of her brother and grandmother. It had been decided that the two households would become one. With that, Yoshiko had made up her mind. She had dreaded marriage on her father's account, but, when it came down to the actual talks, it was not that dreadful after all.

When her preparations were completed, Yoshiko went to her grandmother's room.

"Grandmother, can you see the red in this kimono?"

"I can faintly make out some red over there. Which is it, now?" Pulling Yoshiko to her, the grandmother put her eyes close to the kimono and the sash.

"I've already forgotten your face, Yoshiko. I wish I could see what you look like now."

Yoshiko stifled a desire to giggle. She rested her hand lightly on her grandmother's head.

Wanting to go out and meet her father and the others, Yoshiko was unable just to sit there, vaguely waiting. She went out into the garden. She held out her hand, palm upward, but the rain was so fine that it didn't wet the palm. Gathering up the skirts of her kimono, Yoshiko assiduously searched among the little trees and in the bear-grass bamboo thicket. And there, in the tall grass under the bush clover, was the baby bird.

Her heart beating fast, Yoshiko crept nearer. The baby jay, drawing its head into its neck feathers, did not stir. It was easy to take it up into her hand. It seemed to have lost its energy. Yoshiko looked around her, but the mother bird was nowhere in sight.

Running into the house, Yoshiko called out, "Grandmother! I've found the baby bird. I have it in my hand. It's very weak."

"Oh, is that so? Try giving it some water."

Her grandmother was calm.

When she ladled some water into a rice bowl and dipped the baby jay's beak in it, it drank, its little throat swelling out in an appealing way. Then—had it recovered?—it sang out, "Ki-ki-ki, ki-ki-ki . . ."

The mother bird, evidently hearing its cry, came flying. Perching on the telephone wire, it sang. The baby bird, struggling in Yoshiko's hand, sang out again, "Ki-ki-ki . . ."

"Ah, how good that she came! Give it back to its mother, quick," her grandmother said.

Yoshiko went back out into the garden. The mother bird flew up from the telephone wire but kept her distance, looking fixedly toward Yoshiko from the top of a cherry tree.

As if to show her the baby jay in her palm, Yoshiko raised her hand, then quietly placed the chick on the ground.

As Yoshiko watched from behind the glass door, the mother bird, guided by the voice of its child singing plaintively and looking up at the sky, gradually came closer. When she'd come down to the low branch of a nearby pine, the chick flapped its wings, trying to fly up to her. Stumbling forward in its efforts, falling all over itself, it kept singing.

Still the mother bird cautiously held off from hopping down to the ground.

Soon, however, it flew in a straight line to the side of its child. The chick's joy was boundless. Turning and turning its head, its outspread wings trembling, it made up to its mother. Evidently the mother had brought it something to eat.

Yoshiko wished that her father and stepmother would come soon. She would like to show them this, she thought.

LD

Bamboo-Leaf Boats

[1950]

Akiko placed the bucket beside the hollyhocks. Picking some leaves from the bamboo growing beneath the plum tree, she made several toy boats and floated them on the water in the bucket.

"Look—boats. Aren't they fun?" she said.

A little boy squatted in front of the bucket, peering at the boats. Then he smiled as he looked up at Akiko.

"They're nice boats. Akiko gave you some because you're such a clever boy. Get her to play with you," the boy's mother said as she returned to the parlor.

The woman was also the mother of Akiko's fiancé. Akiko had realized that the woman had something to say to Akiko's father, so she had stepped outside to leave them alone. The boy was so fussy, she had taken him out to the garden with her. The boy was the youngest brother of her fiancé.

The boy stuck his hand in the bucket and stirred the water. "Sister, the boats are having a war." He marveled at the boats whirling about.

Akiko stepped away to wring out a summer kimono that she had been washing. Then she hung it out to dry.

The war was over, but her fiancé had not yet returned.

"Have another war! Another war!" The boy shouted more violently, as he stirred the water. The drops splashed on his face.

"Look at you. Stop that. Your face is all wet." Akiko put an end to his play.

"Now the boats won't go," the boy complained.

The boats really would not move. They merely floated on the surface of the water.

"All right. Let's go to the stream out back. They'll go well there."

The boy took some of the boats. Akiko threw the water at the base of the hollyhocks and returned the bucket to the kitchen.

Akiko and the boy stood on a rock on the bank of the stream. They each let a boat go, and the little boy clapped his hands with glee.

"Look! My boat's in front!"

The boy raced downstream to keep the first boat in sight.

Quickly releasing the rest of the boats, Akiko chased after the boy.

Suddenly Akiko realized that she should make certain to put her left heel all the way to the ground.

Normally, Akiko's left heel no longer touched the ground due to the effects of polio. It was small and tender, and her arch was high. As a child, she was not able to go on field trips or jump rope. She had planned to live her life quietly and alone. But, unexpectedly, arrangements had been made for her to be married. Confident that she could make up for her handicap with willpower, she had begun to practice putting her left heel all the way to the ground more earnestly than she had ever done before. Her left foot had soon become chafed, yet Akiko persevered as though she were doing penance. Since Japan's loss in the war, however, she had quit. The chafe remained, like a severe frostbite scar.

Because the little boy was her fiancé's younger brother, she tried to walk with her left heel on the ground. It had been a long time since she had made the effort.

The stream was narrow, and the weeds that hung into the water from the banks had caught three or four of the boats.

The boy had stopped about ten paces ahead and was watching his boat float away. He did not seem to notice Akiko approaching. He did not see Akiko trying to walk properly.

The deep hollow in the nape of the boy's neck reminded Akiko of her fiancé. She wanted to embrace the boy so much she could hardly stand it.

The boy's mother came out. She thanked Akiko and urged the boy to leave with her.

"Good-bye," the boy said flatly.

Akiko wondered if her fiancé had died in the war or if the engagement had been broken off. Was the offer to marry a cripple just wartime sentimentality?

Akiko did not go inside. Instead, she walked to the new house being built next door. It was a big house, unlike any in the area, so even passersby always stopped to take a look at it. Construction on the house had been stopped during the war, so weeds had grown tall around the stacks of lumber. But now, suddenly, work was progressing again. Two nervous pine trees were planted at the gate.

To Akiko the house looked obstinate, with no gentleness about it. Moreover, there were too many windows. The parlor had windows on all sides.

The neighborhood was gossiping about what kind of people would be moving in, but no one knew for certain.

JMH

Eggs

[1950]

The husband and wife had both caught colds and were sleeping side by side.

The wife always took the older grandchild to bed with her, but her husband hated to be awakened early, so it was rare that they slept side by side.

The husband had caught his cold in a funny way. He had a favorite old hot-spring resort at Tōnosawa in Hakone where he went even in the winter. This year he had gone at the beginning of February. On the third day of his stay, he had hurriedly gotten up and gone to the bath, thinking it was already one-thirty in the afternoon. When he had returned, the maid was putting charcoal in the brazier, looking as though she were half-asleep.

"What's going on this morning? I'm surprised to see you awake so early."

"What? You're being facetious."

"It's still only just past seven. You got up at five after seven."

"What?" He was bewildered. "Oh, I see. I confused the big hand and the little hand on my watch. That's quite a mistake. My eyes are getting old."

"Down at the desk I was worried that a thief or something had gotten into your room."

When he looked up, he saw the maid was wearing a lined *meisen* kimono over her nightgown. Awakened where she slept, she must have had no time to change. He had called the desk to notify them that he was up, but the reason he had gotten no response was that she had been asleep.

"I'm sorry I got you up so early."

"That's all right. It was time to get up anyway. But will you be going back to bed? Shall I get your bedding out again?"

"Well, let me see . . ." He held his hands over the brazier. Now that she mentioned it, he did feel sleepy, but he thought the cold would awaken him.

He had left the inn while the morning was still chilly. And he had caught a cold.

The cause of his wife's cold was not so clear, but colds had been going around, so she had probably caught it from someone else.

By the time the husband had come home, his wife was already in bed.

When the husband had told the story about getting up too early after mistaking the hands of his watch, the whole family had had a good laugh. They had all passed around the pocket watch to have a look at it.

It was a rather large pocket watch; however, they had come to the conclusion that one could confuse the big hand and the little hand in the dim bedside light with sleepy eyes, since the two hands were shaped the same with circles at the tips. They had turned the hands to test whether five after seven could be confused with one-thirty.

"Father needs a watch that glows in the dark," the youngest daughter had said.

Feeling languid and feverish, the husband had decided to sleep beside his wife. "To keep you company," he had said.

"You could probably take the medicine I got for myself from the doctor. After all, we have the same thing."

When they awoke the next morning, the wife asked, "How was Hakone?"

"Well, it was cold," the husband said, summing it all up.

"Last night you coughed terribly and it woke me up, but all I had to do was clear my throat and you started up in a fright. I was quite surprised."

"Really? I didn't know."

"You were sleeping well."

"But I wake up right away if I'm sleeping with our grandson."

"Jumping up startled like that at your age."

"Was I that startled?"

"Yes."

"Maybe it's instinctive, even in a woman my age. If there's a foreign body at your side, you go to sleep and forget, and then—"

" 'Foreign body'? Have I become a 'foreign body'?" Her husband smiled bitterly, but then he added, "That's right. One night in Hakone—I think it was Saturday—a lot of people came to the inn together. After a banquet, one group of guests came to the next room to sleep, but a geisha who had come with them was so dead drunk that her speech was slurred. She was grumbling on the telephone with a geisha in another room. She was screeching and her speech was slurred, so I couldn't understand what she was saying, but it sounded like 'I'm going to lay an egg, I'm going to lay an egg.' It was funny how she said that."

"That's pathetic."

"Pathetic? Her voice was booming."

"Then you looked at your watch, half-asleep, and got up, right?"

"No, stupid." The husband smiled bitterly.

They heard footsteps.

"Mother," the youngest daughter, Akiko, called from beyond the sliding partition, "are you awake?"

"Yes."

"Father, too?"

"Yes, he is."

"May I come in?"

"Yes."

Their fifteen-year-old daughter came in and sat down at her mother's side.

"I had a bad dream."

"What about?"

"I had died. I was a dead person. I knew it was me."

"What a horrible dream!"

"Yes, it was. I was wearing a light kimono, all white. I was going down a straight road. Both sides of the road were foggy. The road seemed to be floating, and I floated when I walked. A strange old woman was following me. She followed me all the way. There was no sound of footsteps. I was so scared I couldn't look back, but I knew she was there. I couldn't get away. Mother, was it the god of death?"

"Of course not," she said as she looked at her husband. "Then what happened?"

"Then, as I walked along, houses began to appear here and there at the roadside. They were low houses like barracks—all the same gray color and all in gentle, rounded shapes. I ducked inside one of the houses. The old woman mistakenly went inside a different house. Good, I thought to myself. But there wasn't anyplace to sleep in the house—just eggs piled everywhere."

"Eggs?" the wife said, exhaling.

"Eggs. I think they were eggs."

"Really? Then what happened?"

"I'm not certain, but I think I was taken up to heaven, away from that house and its eggs. Just as I thought, 'I'm going to heaven,' I woke up."

The girl then looked at her father.

"Father, am I going to die?"

"Of course not." Surprised by her question, he answered the same way his wife had. He had been pondering whether fifteen-year-olds usually have such dreams of death when she had mentioned the eggs. He had almost cried out—it was so bizarre.

"Oh, it was so scary. . . . It still is," the girl said.

"Akiko, yesterday when my throat hurt, I thought it would be good to swallow some raw egg. You went to buy some, and that's why you had the dream about eggs."

"Could that be? Shall I bring you some now? Would you eat some?" The girl went out.

"You were thinking about your good-for-nothing egg geisha, so those eggs appeared in her dream. How pathetic," his wife said.

"Hmm." Her husband was looking at the ceiling. "Does Akiko often dream about death?"

"I don't know. It's the first time, I think."

"Did something happen?"

"I don't know."

"But it was the eggs that made her ascend to heaven, wasn't it?"

Their daughter brought the eggs. She broke one and handed it to her mother. "Here you are," she said, then left the room.

The wife glanced sideways at the egg. "It seems somehow repulsive. I can't swallow it. Here—you take it."

The husband also looked at the egg out of the corner of his eye.

JMH

The Snakes

[1950]

The forty-four-year-old Ineko had a dream.

It was not her own house, it was doubtless some other house that she had gone to, but, when she woke up and thought about it, she could not tell whose house it was. In the dream, Mrs. Kanda, the wife of the company president, had had a proprietary air. Ineko had thought that she was in the Kanda house. But the appearance of the sitting room and the layout of the house were different from the Kandas' place.

When she first saw the little birds, it seemed to Ineko that her husband was also in the room. It seemed as if there were just the two of them.

After he'd heard the story of her dream, her husband had asked, "Were the little birds in a cage? Or did they fly in from the garden?"

Ineko had been at a loss for an answer.

"They were in the sitting room. They were walking around in the sitting room."

There had been two birds, small as hummingbirds and with long tail feathers. Although their bodies were smaller than a long-tail's, their tail feathers were much larger and thicker. They sparkled like jewels.

Ineko had the feeling that their feathers were made out of various jewels. As they moved, beautiful colors and lights shifted delicately in them, just as many precious stones glitter as their facets change and catch the light.

When the birds perched on Ineko's hand and beat their wings, the wings also shone an iridescent color. Within the iridescence, there were five or seven vivid hues.

Other than thinking, "Oh, how pretty," Ineko had felt nothing whatever. It didn't seem strange that a bird with jeweled tail feathers was perched on her hand.

At some point or other, her husband had left the room. Mrs. Kanda was there.

In the room, the ornamental alcove was on the west side. From the south to the east, there was the garden, with a veranda corridor along two sides of the room. At the northeast corner, the corridor turned and became the living room corridor. Ineko and Mrs. Kanda were sitting in that northeast corner, close to the living room.

Five snakes were crawling around the room. When she saw them, Ineko did not cry out but held herself poised to escape.

"It's all right. There's nothing to worry about," Mrs. Kanda said.

Each of the five snakes was a different color. Even after she'd awakened, Ineko clearly remembered those different colors. One snake was a black snake; another was a striped snake; the third was a red snake, like a mountain grass snake; the fourth was patterned like a viper but was a more vivid color; and the fifth was the color of a Mexican fire opal, a terribly pretty snake.

"Ah, how pretty," Ineko thought.

From somewhere or other, Shinoda's previous wife had appeared and was sitting there. Young and lovely, she looked like a dancing girl.

Although Mrs. Kanda seemed to be her actual age and Ineko herself was her own age, Shinoda's previous wife was even younger than when Ineko had known her twenty-five years ago. She seemed to breathe out an air of plump good health.

Shinoda's previous wife was wearing an unpatterned water-green kimono.

Although her clothes were old-fashioned, her coiffure was in the latest style. Gathered forward, it was irritatingly elaborate. A glittering ornament was attached to the front. It was like a large circular comb made of various jewels, or like a small diadem. There were red and green jewels, with a predominance of diamonds.

"My, how pretty."

As Ineko gazed at it, Shinoda's previous wife put a hand to her head and detached the ornament. Holding it out to Ineko, she said, "Won't you buy this from me?"

While she held it in front of Ineko's face, the comblike ornament began slowly, from one end, to undulate. It was, after all, a snake. It was a little snake.

From the living room, there was the sound of running water and the maids' voices. In the far corner of the living room, there was a pantry for tea things. The two maids were washing sweet potatoes.

"Please look carefully at what you buy! Aren't these all too big?" one of the maids said.

The other maid answered, "That's not fair. I picked out the big ones, thinking they were good, and now I get scolded."

At that point, Ineko had woken up.

In the dream, she hadn't taken any particular notice of it, but the garden too was full of snakes.

"Were they crawling around in swarms?"

When her husband had asked this, Ineko had answered precisely, "There were twenty-four of them."

Also, in a separate room behind the sitting room, there had

seemed to be a gathering of menfolk. Mr. Kanda, the company president, was there, along with his younger brother and Ineko's husband. During her dream, Ineko had the feeling, she had heard their voices in conversation.

When Ineko had finished the story of the dream, she and her husband were silent for a while.

"What is Shinoda's previous wife doing these days, I wonder?" her husband finally said.

"Yes, what is she doing?" Ineko echoed.

"I wonder where she is now."

Ineko had not seen her in twenty-five years. It was twenty years or so since Shinoda had died.

Shinoda and Ineko's husband had been classmates at the university. Shinoda's previous wife had made much of Ineko, who was in a lower class at the same girls' school. It was through the wife's good offices that Ineko had gotten married. But before long Shinoda had divorced his first wife and had presently remarried. Since Ineko and her husband had known the second wife as well, the first had come to be called "the previous wife."

The previous wife had dropped out of their sight shortly after the divorce. Shinoda had died three or four years after his remarriage.

Ineko's husband and Shinoda had worked at the same company. The previous wife, interceding with their superior, Kanda, had gotten the jobs for them.

Before marrying Shinoda, the previous wife had been in love with Kanda. But, since Kanda would not marry her, she'd married Shinoda.

Kanda's wife had married him without knowing anything about that. In the past, she had said to Ineko that Shinoda had done a cruel thing to his wife.

Now Kanda had become the company president.

Ineko did not try to force an interpretation on this dream. But she kept it in her heart.

LD

Autumn Rain

[1962]

Deep in my soul I saw a vision of fire falling on mountains red with autumn leaves.

Actually, it was in a valley that I saw it. The valley was deep. The mountains stood high on each side of the riverbank. I could not see the sky above unless I looked straight up. The sky was still blue, but it was tinged with dusk.

The same tinge lay on the white stones of the valley. Did the silence of the autumn colors all around me fill my body, making me feel the dusk early? The valley river flowed a deep indigo; when my eyes marveled that the autumn leaves did not reflect in the deep color of the river, I noticed fire falling into the water.

It did not seem as if the fire rain or fire dust were falling; it merely glittered above the water. But surely it *was* falling; the little bits of fire fell into the indigo water and vanished. I could not see the fire as it fell in front of the mountains because of the red leaves on the mountain trees. So I looked up to check the sky above the mountains and saw small bits of fire falling at a surprising rate. Perhaps because the bits of fire were moving, the narrow strip of sky looked more like a river flowing between the banks formed by the mountain ridges.

Night fell, and this was the vision I had as I dozed off inside an express train bound for Kyoto.

I was on my way to a hotel in Kyoto to see one of two girls who had remained in my memory for fifteen or sixteen years, ever since I was in the hospital for gallstone surgery.

One of them was a baby born without a duct to carry bile. Since such a child would otherwise live only about a year, she had an operation to connect her liver and gallbladder with a man-made tube. I approached her mother as she stood in the hall holding her baby girl. I spoke to her as I looked at the baby. "That all went well. What a pretty child."

"Thank you. The doctor says she won't live past today or tomorrow, so I'm waiting for someone to pick us up from home," her mother said quietly.

The baby slept peacefully. Her camellia kimono bulged out softly at the chest, perhaps because of her bandages from the operation.

My careless remark arose from the relaxed feelings that develop among fellow patients in a hospital, but there were many children who had come to this hospital for heart surgery. Before their surgery they would frolic about the halls and play in the elevator going up and down. I often spoke to those children.

They were from five to seven or eight years old. It is best to repair congenital heart damage while a child is still small. If one does not, the child may die young. One of those children, in particular, attracted my attention. Whenever I got on the elevator, the child was usually there. This five-year-old was always sullen, squatting in the corner of the elevator in the shadow of the adults' legs. She flashed her intense eyes, her obstinate mouth pursed. When I asked the nurse, she said that the girl rode the elevator alone for two or three hours every day. Even when she sat on the sofa in the hall, she had the same angry look. Though I spoke to her, her eyes never changed. "This child will certainly do well," I said to the nurse.

I did not see the girl anymore.

"She was operated on, wasn't she? How did it turn out?" I asked the nurse.

"She went home without having surgery. She saw the child in the bed next to her die, so she said, 'No, I'm going home, I'm going home,' and wouldn't listen to anyone."

"Hmm. But won't she die young?"

I was now on my way to Kyoto to see this girl, now in the prime of her life.

At the sound of rain hitting the window of the train, I awoke from my half-dreaming state. The vision disappeared. I realized that the rain had been striking the window as I had begun to doze off, but it seemed to have grown more intense as the wind now blew the drops loudly against the glass. There were raindrops that traveled from one edge of the window to the other. They stopped a moment, then moved, stopped a moment, then moved. I could see a rhythm as one group of drops moved ahead of another, or as a higher one fell beneath a lower, or as they all flowed together, drawing a single line across the window. I could hear music.

My vision of the fire falling on the autumn mountains had been entirely soundless, but I imagined that it was the music of the drops that struck the glass and flowed along that had become my vision of falling fire.

I had been invited by a dry-goods dealer to a New Year's kimono show to be held at a hall in a Kyoto hotel two days from now. The name of one of the models was Beppu Ritsuko. I had not forgotten that girl's name, but I had not realized that she had become a fashion model. This time I was going to Kyoto more to see Ritsuko than to see the maples.

It was raining the next day, so I was watching television in the lobby in the afternoon. The lobby seemed to be a waiting room for wedding parties; two or three groups of wedding guests were standing around. Brides in full dress also passed through. I occasionally looked behind me to see couples who were being photographed after the ceremonies.

The dry-goods dealer greeted me there. I asked if Beppu Ritsuko was already at the hotel. The dealer immediately motioned me to one side. A young girl was watching intently as a bride and groom were having their picture taken in front of a window clouded by the rain. It was Ritsuko. Her lips were pursed. I drew back and hesitated. I wanted to speak to her, to ask this tall, beautiful girl, who was still living, if she remembered me.

"It's because we're having that girl wear a wedding dress tomorrow," the dealer whispered in my ear.

JMH

The Neighbors

[1962]

"If it's you, the old folks will be happy, too," said Murano, looking at the newlyweds Kichirō and Yukiko. "Both my father and mother are almost completely deaf. It sounds funny to say this, but please don't worry about anything."

For work reasons, Murano had moved to Tokyo. His old father and mother remained at the house in Kamakura. They lived in the detached wing. That was why he was choosing tenants for the main house. Rather than close the house up, it was better to have people living in it. For the old people, too, it was less lonely. The rent was nominal. The go-between in the marriage talks of the young couple, an acquaintance of Murano's, had acted as an intermediary here, also. When Kichirō, with Yukiko, had gone to see Murano, they had been favorably received.

"It'll be like a flower suddenly blooming alongside the old folks. I hadn't been looking especially for newlyweds, but, if I can have you living there, both the old house and the old folks will be bathed in the sunshine of your youth. I can almost see it," Murano said.

The house in Kamakura was at the head of one of the many valleys thereabouts. The main house, with its six rooms, was too large for the young couple. The night of their arrival, unused to the house and the quiet, they turned on all the lights in the six rooms. With lights on even in the kitchen and the earthen entryway, they sat in the twelve-mat parlor. Although it was the largest room in the house, what with Yukiko's armoire, dressing stand, bedding, and the other articles of her dowry that had been brought in here for the time being, there was hardly any room to sit. It made the two feel at home.

Arranging the loose "dragonfly jewels" of her broken necklace in various combinations, Yukiko was trying to piece together a new necklace. Of the two or three hundred of these old glass beads that her father had collected among the natives during his four or five years in Taiwan, Yukiko had been given sixteen or seventeen of her favorites before her marriage. Stringing them together in a necklace, she'd taken them with her on her honeymoon. As her father's prized curios, those dragonfly jewels symbolized for Yukiko the emotion of parting from her parents. The morning after the bridal night, Yukiko had put the necklace on. Attracted by it, Kichirō had embraced Yukiko, pressing his face against her neck. Yukiko, tickled, had pulled away from him with a little scream. The thread of the necklace had snapped. The beads had scattered all over the floor.

"Ahhh!" Kichirō let go of Yukiko. Squatting, the two had gathered up the fallen beads. Yukiko, unable to hold back her laughter at Kichirō crawling around on his hands and knees in search of the beads, suddenly relaxed.

The beads differed in color, pattern, and shape. There were round ones, square ones, and slender tube-shaped ones. The colors—red, blue, purple, yellow, and such—were simple primary colors, and yet, with time, they'd all taken on a subdued, mellow hue. The patterns of the beads, too, had the naive charm of native art. As one subtly varied the arrangement of the beads, the feeling of the necklace also changed subtly. Designed by the natives to be strung on necklaces, each bead had a hole in it for the thread to pass through.

As Yukiko tried changing the arrangement this way and that, Kichirō asked, "Don't you remember the original arrangement?"

"My father and I did it together, so I don't remember everything. I'll string them together in a new way that you like. Please have a look at them."

Shoulder pressed to shoulder, they forgot the passage of time in the arrangement of the dragonfly jewels. The night grew late.

"Isn't something walking around outside?" Yukiko listened. There was the scurrying sound of dead leaves. Leaves seemed to be falling, not on the roof of this house, but on the roof of the detached wing in back. The wind had risen.

The next morning, Yukiko called out to Kichirō.

"Come here, come here quickly! The old folks in back are feeding a couple of black kites. The kites are having breakfast with them."

When Kichirō got up and went outside, he saw that the doors of the detached wing were all open in the mild, clear autumn daylight. In the sun that shone into the breakfast room, the old husband and wife were having their breakfast. The detached wing stood on a slight rise from the garden, set off from it by a low hedge of mountain tea flower. Since the hedge was in full bloom, the detached wing seemed to float above a bank of flowers. On three sides it was surrounded, as if about to be buried, by the mixed forest of the low mountain in its fall colors. The late-autumn morning sunlight, shining through the tea-flower hedge and the fall foliage, seemed to warm them to their innermost depths.

The two kites, approaching the breakfast table, lifted their heads. The old couple, chewing up the ham and omelet on their plates, held it out to them between their chopsticks. Each time they did so, the birds would spread their wings a little.

"They're so tame," Kichirō said. "Let's go over and say hello. It's during breakfast, but I don't think they'll mind. I'd like to meet their beloved birds."

Going inside, Yukiko changed into day clothes. When she came out, she was wearing the necklace they'd worked on so hard the night before.

At the sound of their approach to the tea-flower hedge, the two birds suddenly took flight. Their beating wings startled the young couple's ears. Exclaiming "Ahh," Yukiko looked up as the kites ascended into the sky. Evidently they were mountain kites who had come down to the old folks' place.

Painstakingly expressing their gratitude at being allowed to live in the main house, Kichirō said, "I'm sorry I scared the birds away. They've certainly taken to you."

But the old people didn't seem to have heard anything. Apparently not even trying to hear, they gazed emptily at the young couple. Turning to Kichirō, Yukiko asked him with her eyes what to do.

"It was very good of you to come. Mother—this beautiful young couple are our neighbors now." The old man spoke abruptly, as if to himself. But his wife didn't seem to hear this either.

"Old deaf folks like us—you can think of us as not being here. But we like to see young people. We won't make any trouble for you, but we won't hide ourselves away."

Kichirō and Yukiko bowed their heads.

A kite was circling high over the roof of the cottage. It cried out with a sweet voice.

"The kites haven't finished their breakfast. They've come down from the mountain again. We mustn't be in their way." Kichirō, urging Yukiko, got to his feet.

LD

Up in the Tree

[1962]

Keisuke's house was on the shore where the great river began to enter the sea. Although the river ran alongside the garden, because of the somewhat elevated embankment it could not be seen from the house. The old shore, lined with pines and slightly lower than the embankment, seemed part of the garden, its pines the garden pines. This side of the pines, there was a hedge of Chinese black pine.

Michiko, forcing her way through the hedge, came to play with Keisuke. No, she came just to be with him. Both Michiko and Keisuke were fourth graders. This ducking through the hedge, instead of coming in by the front gate or by the garden gate in back, was a secret between them. For a girl, it wasn't easy. Shielding her head and face with both arms, bent over from the waist, she would plunge into the hedge. Tumbling out into the garden, she would often be caught up in Keisuke's arms.

Shy about letting the people in the house know that Michiko came every day, Keisuke had taught her this way through the hedge.

"I like it. My heart pounds and pounds like anything," Michiko said.

One day, Keisuke climbed up into a pine tree. While he was up there, along came Michiko. Looking neither right nor left, she hurried along by the shore. Stopping at the hedge where she always went through, she looked all around her. Bringing her long, triple-braided pigtails in front of her face, she put them into her mouth halfway along their length. Bracing herself, she threw herself at the hedge. Up in the tree, Keisuke held his breath. When she'd popped out of the hedge into the garden, Michiko did not see Keisuke, whom she had thought would be there. Frightened, she shrank back into the shadow of the hedge, where Keisuke could not see her.

"Mitchan, Mitchan," Keisuke called. Michiko, coming away from the hedge, looked around the garden.

"Mitchan, I'm in the pine tree. I'm up in the pine tree." Looking up toward Keisuke's voice, Michiko did not say a word. Keisuke said, "Come out. Come out of the garden."

When Michiko had come back out through the hedge, she looked up at Keisuke.

"You come down."

"Mitchan, climb up here. It's nice up here in the tree."

"I can't climb it. You're making fun of me, just like a boy. Come down."

"Come up here. The branches are big like this, so even a girl can do it."

Michiko studied the branches. Then she said, "If I fall, it's your fault. If I die, I won't know anything about it."

First dangling from a lower branch, she began to climb.

By the time she'd gotten up to Keisuke's branch, Michiko was gasping for breath. "I climbed it, I climbed it." Her eyes sparkled. "It's scary. Hold me."

"Hmm." Keisuke firmly drew Michiko to him.

Michiko, her arms around Keisuke's neck, said, "You can see the ocean."

"You can see everything. Across the river, and even up the river . . . It's good you climbed up here."

"It *is* good. Keichan, let's climb up here tomorrow."

"Hmm." Keisuke was silent a while. "Mitchan, it's a secret. Climbing up the tree and being up here in the tree—it's a secret. I read books and do homework up here. It's no good if you tell anyone."

"I won't tell." Michiko bowed her head in assent. "Why have you become like a bird?"

"Since it's you, Mitchan, I'll tell you. My father and mother had an awful quarrel. My mother said she was going to take me and go back to her parents' house. I didn't want to look at them, so I climbed a tree in the garden and hid at the top. Saying, 'Where's Keisuke gone to?' they looked all over for me. But they couldn't find me. From the tree, I saw my father go all the way to the ocean to look. This was last spring."

"What were they quarreling about?"

"Don't you know? My father has a woman."

Michiko said nothing.

"Since then, I've been up in the trees a lot. My father and mother still don't know. It's a secret," Keisuke said again, just to make sure. "Mitchan, starting tomorrow, bring your schoolbooks. We'll do our homework up here. We'll get good grades. The trees in the garden are all those big camellia trees with lots of leaves, so nobody can see us from the ground or anywhere."

The "secret" of their being up in the tree had continued for almost two years now. Where the thick trunk branched out near the top, the two could sit comfortably. Michiko, straddling one branch, leaned back against another. There were days when little birds came and days when the wind sang through the pine needles. Although they weren't that high off the ground, these two little lovers felt as if they were in a completely different world, far away from the earth.

LD

Riding Clothes

[1962]

When she arrived at the hotel in London, Nagako drew the curtains tightly shut and lay down as if collapsing on the bed. She closed her eyes. She'd forgotten even to take off her shoes. Pushing her feet out over the edge of the bed, she shook them. The shoes obligingly dropped off.

Her weariness was more than that of the solitary flight by the polar route over Alaska and Denmark. It was as if that weariness had allowed the other—the weariness of her life as a woman, the weariness of her marriage with Iguchi—to surface suddenly.

A continual warbling of little birds reached her ear. The hotel was in a quiet residential section beside Holland Park. Probably there were many little birds in the groves of the park. Although the season was not as far along as in Tokyo, still it was May: Trees were leafing, flowers blossoming, and little birds singing. It was the London spring. But the window was closed, the curtains drawn, the outside invisible. When she heard the little birds, Nagako did not feel as if she had come to a distant country.

"This is London, in England." Even when she told herself this, Nagako felt as if she were in the uplands of Japan. By the birds' warbling, it might well have been the mountains, but it was the uplands that came into her mind because she had happy memories of the uplands.

The twelve- or thirteen-year-old Nagako, with her uncle

and cousins, was riding on horseback along a green road in the uplands. That little figure of herself came into view. Even after she'd been taken into her uncle's bright, cheerful house, Nagako could clearly recall the darkness of her life with her father. When she rode fast on horseback, she forgot all about her father's death. But her happiness was short-lived.

"Nagako. He's your cousin. It's no good."

Her cousin Shigeko broke in on her happiness with these words. Nagako, who had turned fourteen, knew what the words meant. She was being warned that love and marriage with her cousin Yosuke were "no good."

Nagako loved to cut Yosuke's toenails and fingernails for him and to clean his ears. She was happy when he told her she was good at it. Nagako's selfless air when she did things for Yosuke had irritated Shigeko. After that, Nagako had kept her distance from Yosuke. She was much younger than he, and she had not even dreamed of marrying him. But her heart, the heart of a young woman, had been awakened by Shigeko's words. Long afterward, she thought of her feelings for Yosuke as first love.

Yosuke had married and set up his own household, Shigeko had married and gone away, and Nagako had remained at home. Thinking even that would displease Shigeko, she'd gone to live in the dormitory at a women's college. Her uncle had arranged a marriage. When her husband had lost his job, Nagako had taken a position as English instructor at a preparatory school. Finally, Nagako had approached her uncle about a divorce.

"It seems to me that Iguchi is becoming exactly like my father," Nagako had complained of her husband. "If my father hadn't been that way, I might have put up with Iguchi. But, when I think of my father, I have the feeling that I'm dogged by a fate of living with weak, ineffectual men. I just can't stand it."

Her uncle, who bore the responsibility for her marriage to Iguchi, looked at the agitated Nagako. Then, saying she should try leaving Japan for a while, stay in England for three weeks or a month and think the thing through, he'd given her money for the trip.

In the hotel in London, listening to the warbling of the birds, remembering the little figure of herself on horseback, Nagako began to hear a ringing in her ears. It became the rushing noise of a waterfall. The sound of the torrent grew to a roar. About to cry out, Nagako opened her eyes.

Nagako, bearing a letter from her father, timidly entered the company director's office on the seventh floor. The director, who'd been an upper school classmate of her father's, looked at Nagako.

"How old are you?"

"Eleven."

"Hmm. Please tell your father he shouldn't use his own child for this kind of thing. A child . . . It's pathetic."

Grimacing, the director had given her some money.

Nagako repeated the director's words to her father, who was waiting for her on the sidewalk. Tottering as he shook his cane at the window above, her father cursed.

"That bastard. A waterfall's coming down on my head. It's battering me to death." It truly seemed to Nagako that a torrential waterfall was pouring down on her father's head from the seventh-floor window.

Nagako had taken letters from her father to three or four companies. At each company, there was a director who'd been a classmate of her father's. Nagako went around to them in turn.

Her mother, disgusted with her father, left him. After a slight stroke, her father could not get around without a cane. About a month after the visit to the company of the waterfall, Nagako went to another company.

The director said, "You didn't come by yourself. Where's your father hiding?" Nagako's eyes went to the window. The director, opening the window, looked down. "Here, what's this?"

Drawn by his voice, Nagako looked out the window. Her father had fallen in the street. A crowd had collected. It was his second stroke. Her father was dead. Nagako felt as if the waterfall, plunging from the high office window, had struck and killed her father.

In her room at the London hotel where she had just now arrived, Nagako heard the sound of that waterfall.

On Sunday, Nagako went for a walk in Hyde Park. Sitting on a bench beside a pond, she gazed at the waterfowl. At the sound of hoofbeats, she turned her head. A family on horseback approached, parents and children alongside each other. Even the girl, about ten, and her brother, who seemed two or three years older, were dressed in correct riding clothes. Nagako was surprised. They were picture perfect, the little lady and the little gentleman. Watching the family group gallop past, Nagako thought she would like to find a shop in London that sold that kind of well-cut riding clothes and at least touch them.

LD

Immortality

[1963]

An old man and a young girl were walking together.

There were a number of curious things about them. They nestled close together like lovers, as if they did not feel the sixty years' difference in their ages. The old man was hard of hearing. He could not understand most of what the girl said. The girl wore maroon *hakama* with a purple-and-white kimono in a fine arrow pattern. The sleeves were rather long. The old man was wearing clothes like those a girl would wear to pull weeds from a rice field, except that he wore no leggings. His tight sleeves and trousers gathered at the ankles looked like a woman's. His clothes hung loose at his thin waist.

They walked across a lawn. A tall wire net stood in front of them. The lovers did not seem to notice that they would run into it if they kept walking. They did not stop, but walked right through the net as a spring breeze might blow through it.

After they passed through, the girl noticed the net. "Oh." She looked at the man. "Shintarō, did you pass through the net, too?"

The old man did not hear, but he grabbed the wire net. "You bastard. You bastard," he said as he shook it. He pulled too hard, and in a moment, the huge net moved away from him. The old man staggered and fell holding on to it.

"Watch out, Shintarō! What happened?" The girl put her arms around him and propped him up.

"Let go of the net . . . Oh, you've lost so much weight," the girl said.

The old man finally stood up. He heaved as he spoke. "Thank you." He grasped the net again, but this time lightly, with only one hand. Then in the loud voice of a deaf person he said, "I used to have to pick up balls from behind a net day after day. For seventeen long years."

"Seventeen years is a long time? . . . It's short."

"They just hit the balls as they pleased. They made an awful sound when they struck the wire net. Before I got used to it, I'd flinch. It's because of the sound of those balls that I became deaf."

It was a metal net to protect the ball boys at a golf driving range. There were wheels on the bottom so they could move forward and back and right and left. The driving range and golf course next to it were separated by some trees. Originally it had been a grove of all kinds of trees, but they had been cut until only an irregular row remained.

The two walked on, the net behind them.

"What pleasant memories it brings back to hear the sound of the ocean." Wanting the old man to hear these words, the girl put her mouth to his ear. "I can hear the sound of the ocean."

"What?" The old man closed his eyes. "Ah, Misako. It's your sweet breath. Just as it was long ago."

"Can't you hear the sound of the ocean? Doesn't it bring back fond memories?"

"The ocean . . . Did you say the ocean? Fond memories? How could the ocean, where you drowned yourself, bring back fond memories?"

"Well, it does. This is the first time I've been back to my hometown in fifty-five years. And you've come back here, too. This brings back memories." The old man could not hear, but she went on. "I'm glad I drowned myself. That way I can think about you forever, just as I was doing at the moment I drowned myself. Besides, the only memories and reminiscences I have are those up to the time I was eighteen. You are eternally young to me. And it's the same for you. If I hadn't drowned myself and you came to the village now to see me, I'd be an old woman. How disgusting. I wouldn't want you to see me like that."

The old man spoke. It was a deaf man's monologue. "I went to Tokyo and failed. And now, decrepit with age, I've returned to the village. There was a girl who grieved that we were forced to part. She had drowned herself in the ocean, so I asked for a job at a driving range overlooking the ocean. I begged them to give me the job . . . if only out of pity."

"This area where we are walking is the woods that belonged to your family."

"I couldn't do anything but pick up balls. I hurt my back from bending over all the time . . . But there was a girl who had killed herself for me. The rock cliffs were right beside me, so I could jump even if I were tottering. That's what I thought."

"No. You must keep living. If you were to die, there wouldn't be anyone on earth who would remember me. I would die completely." The girl clung to him. The old man could not hear, but he embraced her.

"That's it. Let's die together. This time . . . You came for me, didn't you."

"Together? But you must live. Live for my sake, Shintarō." She gasped as she looked over his shoulder. "Oh, those big trees are still there. All three . . . just like long ago." The girl pointed, so the old man turned his eyes toward the trees.

"The golfers are afraid of those trees. They keep telling us to cut them down. When they hit a ball, they say it curves to the right as though sucked in by the magic of those trees."

"Those golfers will die in due time—long before those trees. Those trees are already hundreds of years old. Those golfers talk that way, but they don't understand the life span of a man," the girl said.

"Those are trees my ancestors have looked after for hundreds of years, so I had the buyer promise not to cut the trees when I sold the land to him."

"Let's go." The girl tugged at the old man's hand. They tottered toward the great trees.

The girl passed easily through the tree trunk. The old man did the same.

"What?" The girl stared at the old man and marveled. "Are you dead too, Shintarō? Are you? When did you die?"

He did not answer.

"You *have* died . . . Haven't you? How strange I didn't meet you in the world of the dead. Well, try walking through the tree trunk once more to test whether you're dead or alive. If you are dead we can go inside the tree and stay."

They disappeared inside the tree. Neither the old man nor the young girl appeared again.

The color of evening began to drift onto the small saplings behind the great trees. The sky beyond turned a faint red where the ocean sounded.

JMH

Earth

[1963]

"A woman clothed with the sun, and the moon under her feet, and upon her head a crown of twelve stars: And she being with child cried travailing in birth and pained to be delivered."

2

"Before I knew it, a small Catholic church had been built beside the road that ran alongside the waterwheel, the road where I had enjoyed walking long ago. Moreover, the beautiful unfinished wooden walls of the church were already blackened by charcoal soot, under the steep, snow-covered roof." This is written in one of Hori Tatsuo's stories. The roof of Saint Paul's Church was shingled, and inside it resembled praying hands. Of course, the cross on the altar was also made of wood.

3

Now, when these words that Hori Tatsuo had written were already twenty-five years old, a young man and woman were walking in clothes like those one would see in Karuizawa during the summer at midday.

"It was while passing in front of this church that my mother was told something dreadful." The young man stopped walking and looked at the church as he spoke to the young woman. She also looked at the church; then she looked at the young man's face.

"But you believe your mother. Because you believe your mother, you have a definite father."

The young man did not speak.

"I'm a child without a father who has no way to believe her mother—a child with absolutely no father," she went on.

"It's not like you can know your father by believing your mother. If the father doesn't believe the mother, if your father also doubts your mother, then there is no end to the doubting."

"But, for example, even if you were to doubt, you *have* a father whom you can doubt. I don't have a father even in illusion. I wonder if the prison itself was my father."

"I don't have a single thing about me that resembles my father."

"That's right. You don't. And you don't resemble your mother at all, either."

"Why would that be?"

4

"It's not my child. Who knows whose child it might be."

These were the dreadful words that the young man's mother heard from her husband when she announced that she was pregnant. They were walking in front of the church more than twenty years earlier.

The young woman, who had known only one man, was overcome with shock and fear. She could not even find the strength to swear her fidelity. If her husband were to reject her testimony, she had no other recourse.

As evidence, the young woman took the baby she had borne to her husband's house to show him.

"It's not my child. Who knows whose child it might be." Again he rejected the baby. "It's the child of adultery."

The young woman lost her head and moved to stab the baby with a mountain climber's knife that was lying nearby. The young man snatched the child from his wife and tripped her. Then she stabbed the baby's father.

At that moment, the vision of a painting flashed into the heart of the chaste wife, as though illuminated by lightning. It was a mural in an old underground chapel, which warned against adultery. Two white snakes hung from a woman's breasts, biting them. A spear was driven through one of the woman's breasts and into her chest by Christ's hand: Christ had killed the woman with a spear. The girl screamed.

The husband's wound was severe. Rather than forgive the girl, he and his family reported everything. So the woman was arrested.

5

While the girl was among the inmates in the prison, the heavens opened and she saw a vision of God.

6

While she was in prison, another young woman was admitted; this young woman had killed her lover in a fit of jealousy. When she learned that the girl had a child, she envied her intensely.

"I wanted to have his baby, but now I can't—I killed him." She clung to the girl and cried. "I can't. Never in my whole life. I can't have anyone's child. I'll be in prison until I'm too old to have a child. That's the death penalty for a woman. When I think of it, I want to have a baby—anyone's baby, any way I can."

"Any way you can?"

"Anyone's child."

"Really? If that's true, shall I make you have one?"

"Aren't you a woman?"

"I'll be out of here soon. Wait until then. I'll make you have a child."

7

After the girl was released from prison, she returned to visit the woman left behind.

The woman in prison became pregnant.

This created quite a stir throughout the prison: The woman would not confess whose child it was. There was no way she could even begin to try. The guards and other men in the prison were all interrogated, but the guards for the female prisoners were all women. There were no men who came near the women. And there was no way she could have gone outside the prison.

The nun who was the prison chaplain did not say it was a miracle, or the Holy Ghost, or that a son of God would be born.

Filled with peace, the woman nursed the baby girl in prison. She wrote a letter of thanks to her friend.

The other young woman did not come to see her a second time.

8

The baby girl was adopted and grew up happy. She was the girl who was now walking in front of Saint Paul's Church. Anytime she wanted, she could see her real mother, who was now out of prison. She had heard the story of her own birth behind bars.

The young man walking with her was the child whom his

mother had tried to kill. His father had eventually forgiven his mother. They were reconciled and were still together.

"Because the one who saved me and was himself wounded was my father?" the young man mused.

"That's right." The girl nodded. "And I, who was a child with no father, shall bear a child with a father."

The young man also nodded as they walked down the road in front of the church.

9

"And the serpent cast out of his mouth water as a flood after the woman, that he might cause her to be carried away of the flood. And the earth helped the woman, and the earth opened her mouth, and swallowed up the flood which the dragon cast out of his mouth."

JMH

The White Horse

[1963]

In the leaves of the oak tree, there was a silver sun.

Raising his face, Noguchi was dazzled by the light. He blinked and looked again. The light was not directly striking his eyes; it was caught amid the dense foliage.

For a Japanese oak, the tree had much too thick a trunk and stood much too tall. A number of other oaks clustered around it. Their lower branches unpruned, they screened the western sun. Beyond the stand of oaks, the summer sun went on sinking.

Because of the thickly intermeshed foliage, the sun itself could not be seen. Instead, the sun was the light that spread itself among the leaves. Noguchi was used to seeing it that way. On the highlands, the green of the leaves was as vivid as that of a Western oak. Absorbing the light, the leaves of the oak turned to a pale, translucent green and made sparkling wavelets of light as they swayed in the breeze.

This evening, the leaves of the tree were quiet. The light on the foliage was still.

"What?" Noguchi said the word out loud. He had just noticed the dusky color of the sky. It was not the color of a sky in which the sun was still halfway up in the high stand of oaks. It was the color of a sky in which the sun had just set. The silvery light on the oak leaves came from a small white cloud beyond the grove that reflected the light of the setting sun. To the left of the grove, the faraway waves of mountains were darkening to a deep, faded blue.

The silvery light, which had been caught by the grove, suddenly went out. The green of the thick foliage slowly blackened. From the summit of the trees, a white horse leapt upward and galloped across the gray sky.

"Ahh . . ." But Noguchi was not that surprised. It was not an unusual dream for him.

"She's riding it again, in a black robe again."

The black robe of the woman astride the horse streamed out behind her. No—the folds of long black cloth that flowed over the stallion's arched tail were attached to the robe but seemed separate from it.

"What is it?" As Noguchi was thinking this, the vision faded away. But the rhythm of the horse's legs remained in his heart. Although the horse seemed to gallop headlong like a racehorse, there was a leisurely rhythm in the gallop. And the legs were the only part of the horse in motion. The hooves were sharply pointed.

"That long black cloth in back of her—what was it? Or was it a cloth?" Noguchi asked himself uneasily.

When Noguchi had been in the upper grades of elementary school, he had played with Taeko in the garden where the sweet oleander hedge was in bloom. They had drawn pictures together. They drew pictures of horses; when Taeko drew a horse galloping across the sky, Noguchi drew one, too.

"That's the horse that stamped on the mountain and made the sacred spring gush up," Taeko said.

"Shouldn't he have wings?" Noguchi asked. The horse he'd drawn was winged.

"He doesn't need any," Taeko answered, "because he has sharp hooves."

"Who is riding him?"

"Taeko. Taeko is riding him. She's riding the white horse and wearing pink clothes."

"Oh, so Taeko's riding the horse that stamped on the mountain and made the sacred spring gush up."

"That's right. Your horse has wings, but nobody's riding him."

"Here, then." Noguchi hurriedly drew a boy atop the horse. Taeko looked on from the side.

That was all there had been. Noguchi had married another girl, had fathered children, had aged, had forgotten about that kind of thing.

He'd remembered it suddenly, late one sleepless night. His son, having failed his university entrance tests, was studying every night until two or three o'clock. Noguchi, worried about him, could not get to sleep. As the sleepless nights continued, Noguchi came up against the loneliness of life. The son had next year, had hope, did not even go to bed at night. But the father merely lay awake in his bed. It was not for his son's sake. He was experiencing his own loneliness. Once he had been caught by this loneliness, it did not let him go. It put down its roots in the deepest part of him.

Noguchi tried various ways to fall asleep. He tried thinking of quiet fantasies and memories. And, one night, unexpectedly, he remembered Taeko's picture of the white horse. He did not clearly recall the picture. It was no child's picture, but the vision of a white horse galloping through heaven that floated up behind Noguchi's closed eyelids in the dark.

"Is it Taeko riding him? In pink clothes?"

The figure of the white horse, galloping across the sky, was clear. But neither the form nor the color of the rider astride him was clear. It did not seem to be a girl.

As the speed with which the visionary steed galloped through the empty sky slackened and the vision faded away, Noguchi would be drawn down into sleep.

From that night on, Noguchi had used the vision of the

white horse as an invitation to sleep. His sleeplessness became a frequent occurrence, a customary thing whenever he suffered or was anxious.

For several years now, Noguchi had been saved from his insomnia by the vision of the white horse. The imaginary white horse was vivid and lively, but the figure riding him seemed to be a woman in black. It was not a girl in pink. The figure of that black-robed woman, aged and weakened, grew mysterious as time went by.

Today was the first time that the dream of the white horse had come to Noguchi, not as he lay in bed with his eyes closed, but as he sat open-eyed in a chair. It was the first time, also, that something like a long black cloth had streamed out behind the woman. Although it flowed in the wind, the drapery was thick and heavy.

"What is it?"

Noguchi gazed at the darkening gray sky from which the vision of the white horse had faded.

He had not seen Taeko in forty years. There was no news of her.

LD

Snow

[1964]

For the past four or five years, Noda Sankichi had secluded himself at a Tokyo high-rise hotel from the evening of New Year's Day until the morning of the third. Although the hotel had an imposing name, Sankichi's name for it was the Dream Hotel.

"Father has gone to the Dream Hotel," his son or his daughter would say to New Year's visitors who came to the house. The visitors would take it as a joke meant to conceal Sankichi's whereabouts.

"That's a nice place. He must be having a good New Year's there." Some of them even said this.

However, not even Sankichi's family knew that Sankichi actually did have dreams at the Dream Hotel.

The room at the hotel was the same every year. It was the Snow Room. Again, only Sankichi knew that he always called whatever room it was the Snow Room.

When he'd arrived at the hotel, Sankichi would draw the curtains of the room, immediately get into bed, and close his eyes. For two or three hours, he would lie there quietly. It was true that he was seeking rest from the irritation and fatigue of a busy, agitated year, but, even when the fretful tiredness had gone away, a deeper weariness welled up and spread out within him. Understanding this, Sankichi waited for his weariness to reach its fullest extent. When he had been pulled down to the bottom of the weariness, his head gone numb with it, then the dream would begin to rise toward the surface.

In the darkness behind his eyelids, tiny millet-sized grains of light would begin to dance and flow. The grains were of a pale, golden, transparent hue. As their gold chilled to a faint whiteness, they turned into snowflakes, all flowing in the same direction and at the same slow speed. They were powdery flakes, falling in the distance.

"This New Year's, too, the snow has come."

With this thought, the snow would belong to Sankichi. It was falling in Sankichi's heart.

In the darkness of his closed eyes, the snow came nearer. Falling thick and fast, it changed into peony snowflakes. The big, petal-like snowflakes fell more slowly than the powdery snowflakes. Sankichi was enfolded in the silent, peaceful blizzard.

It was all right to open his eyes now.

When Sankichi opened his eyes, the wall of the room had become a snowscape. What he'd seen behind his eyelids was merely the snow falling; what he saw on the wall was the landscape in which the snow had fallen.

In a large field in which stood only five or six bare-branched trees, peony snowflakes were falling. As the snow drifted higher, neither earth nor grass was visible. There were no houses, no sign of a human being. It was a lonely scene, and yet Sankichi, in his electrically heated bed, did not feel the coldness of the snowy field. But the snowy landscape was all there was. Sankichi himself was not there.

"Where shall I go? Whom shall I call?" Although the thought came to him, it was not his own. It was the voice of the snow.

The snowy plain, in which nothing moved but falling snow, presently, of its own accord, flowed away, shifting to the scenery of a mountain gorge. On the far side, the mountain towered up.

A stream wound along its base. Although the narrow stream seemed choked with snow, it was flowing without a ripple. A mass of snow that had fallen in from the bank was floating along. Halted by a boulder that jutted out into the current, it melted into the water.

The boulder was a huge mass of amethyst quartz.

At the top of the quartz boulder, Sankichi's father appeared. His father was holding the three- or four-year-old Sankichi in his arms.

"Father, it's dangerous—standing on that sort of sharp, jagged rock. The soles of your feet must hurt." From the bed, the fifty-four-year-old Sankichi spoke to his father in the snowy landscape.

The crown of the boulder was a cluster of pointed quartz crystals that looked as if they could pierce his father's feet. At Sankichi's words, his father shifted his weight for a better footing. As he did so, the snow atop the boulder crumbled and fell into the stream. Perhaps frightened by that, Sankichi's father held him tighter.

"It's strange that this narrow little stream isn't buried under so much snow," his father said.

There was snow on his father's head and shoulders and on his arms, which held Sankichi.

The snow scene on the wall was shifting, moving upstream. A lake came into view. It was a small lake, in the depths of the mountains, but, as the source of such a narrow little stream, it seemed too large. The white peony snowflakes, the farther away they were, took on a tinge of gray. Heavy clouds hovered in the distance. The mountains on the far shore were indistinct.

Sankichi gazed for a while at the steadily falling peony snowflakes as they melted into the lake's surface. On the mountains of the far shore, something was moving. It was coming nearer through the gray sky. It was a flock of birds. They had great snow-colored wings. As if the snow itself had become their wings, even when they flew past Sankichi's eyes, there was no sound of wingbeats. Were their wings extended in silent, slow waves? Was the falling snow bearing up the birds?

When he tried to count the birds, there were seven, there were eleven . . . He lost count. But Sankichi felt it as a pleasure rather than as a puzzlement.

"What birds are those? What are those wings?"

"We're not birds. Don't you see who's riding on the wings?" A voice answered from one of the snowbirds.

"Ah, I see," Sankichi said.

Riding on the birds through the falling snow, all the women who had loved Sankichi had come to him. Which of them had spoken first?

In his dream, Sankichi could freely call up those who had loved him in the past.

From the evening of New Year's Day to the morning of the third, in the Snow Room of the Dream Hotel, drawing the curtains, having his meals brought to the room, never leaving his bed, Sankichi communed with those souls.

LD

Gleanings from Snow Country

[1972]

After the long border tunnel, the snow country appeared. The depths of the night became white. The train stopped at the signal.

A girl stood up from the seat opposite and opened the window in front of Shimamura. The snowy cold flowed in. The girl hung out of the window and called out as if to the distance, "Stationmaster! Stationmaster!"

The man came tramping across the snow carrying a lantern. He wore his muffler up around his nose, and the flaps of his cap hung over his ears.

Shimamura gazed outside. Is it that cold? Barracks that may have been housing for road employees were scattered across the foot of the mountain, but the white of the snow was swallowed up in darkness before it reached them.

Some three hours earlier, to dispel his boredom, Shimamura had gazed at the forefinger of his left hand as he wiggled it. In the end, it was only this finger that vividly remembered the woman he was on his way to meet. The more he endeavored to recall her clearly, the more uncanny it seemed that this finger alone should be moist now with her touch and be drawing him to the distant woman even as she faded from the grasp of his uncertain memory. He brought the finger to his nose and tried smelling it, then drew a line across the window glass with the finger. A woman's eye appeared there. He was so startled he almost cried out, but that was because his mind had been elsewhere. When he came to himself he realized it was nothing, just the reflection of the girl in the seat on the opposite side of the car. Darkness had fallen outside, and the lights were on inside the train: the glass of the window had become a mirror. But it had been fogged over with water vapor, so the mirror had not appeared until he wiped it with his finger.

The evening scene flowed in the depths of the mirror. The mirror itself and the objects reflected in it moved like a double-exposed motion picture, with no connection between the actors and the scene. Moreover, as the actor, with mutable transparency, and the scene, with its misty flow—as the two fused together, they depicted an unearthly world of symbols. Especially when the lights in the fields and mountains shined in the middle of the girl's face, his heart fluttered with the inexpressible beauty.

The distant sky above the mountains still bore traces of the sunset, so he could make out the shapes in the scenery through the window even in the distance, although the colors had faded. As far as he could see, the landscape of ordinary mountains and fields appeared all the more ordinary. Nothing stood out and nothing attracted his attention, so it was more like a great flow of emotion. Naturally, that was because the girl's eye floated in the midst of it. The evening scenery continued to move past the girl's lovely profile in the window mirror, so the girl's face, too, appeared transparent. But, he could not catch a long enough glance to see if it was part of the scenery that flowed ceaselessly behind, since the girl's face appeared to pass before it.

The train was not very light inside and the window was not

so powerful as a real mirror. There was no other reflection, so Shimamura gradually forgot that there was a mirror as he was peering into it. He began to imagine that the girl was floating in the evening landscape.

Then a light burned in the middle of her face; the reflected image was not strong enough to eliminate the light from outside, and the light did not obliterate the reflection. So the light drifted across the girl's face, but it did nothing to illuminate or brighten her. It was a cold, distant light. As it shined about her pupil—in other words, in the instant when the light and the girl's eye were superimposed—her eye was transformed into a beautiful, bewitching, glowing insect that floated on the waves of the night darkness.

Before the beginning of the ski season, the hot-spring inn had its fewest guests. The whole inn was already asleep when Shimamura got out of the bath. Every time he took a step along the ancient hallway, the glass doors rattled faintly. At the corner far down the hall near the desk, the woman stood, the skirts of her kimono spread over the dark, lustrous, cold wooden floor.

Has she become a geisha? He was startled when he saw the skirts of her kimono. She did not approach him, nor did she relax her posture to greet him. Even at a distance Shimamura perceived something grave in her figure as she stood motionless. He hurried toward her. Her white made-up face turned to tears when she tried to smile, so they began to walk toward his room silently.

In spite of what had happened between them, Shimamura had not written or come to see her or even kept his promise to send her the book of dance instructions. Surely the woman could only imagine that she had been forgotten, so it was now

Shimamura's place to apologize or offer an excuse. But even as they walked, not looking at each other's faces, Shimamura realized that, far from attacking him, the woman's whole body was filled with longing for what she once had felt, so he thought that any words he might speak now would only have a frivolous ring to them. He was wrapped in the sweet joy that the woman would have her way. Then at the foot of the stairs he suddenly thrust out his left hand in front of the woman, his index finger extended. "This is what remembered you best."

"Oh?" the woman said as she grasped the finger and pulled as she ascended the stairs. When she let go in front of the charcoal brazier, she blushed lightly to her neck, but she lifted his hand again so he would not notice. "So this remembered me?"

"Not the right—this one." He slipped his right hand from between her palms and held out his left fist.

Her face was clear. "Yes, I see." Stifling a smile, she spread Shimamura's fingers and pressed her face against his palm. "Did this remember me?"

"Oh, it's cold. I've never felt your hair so cold."

"It still hasn't snowed in Tokyo, has it?"

Shimamura stood in the entryway and looked up at the mountain behind the inn where the scent of the new leaves was strong. He scrambled up the mountain as if lured by it. What was it that was so amusing? All alone, he did not stop laughing.

After a while, tired out, he turned around, hiked up his summer kimono, and bounded down the slope. Two yellow butterflies flew up from his feet.

As the butterflies flew off, weaving in and out, they soon were so far away above the border mountains that their yellow turned to whiteness.

"What have you been doing?" The woman was standing in the shadows of a cedar grove. "You were laughing so joyfully."

"I quit." The senseless laughter rose again. "I quit."

"Really?" The woman looked away and walked slowly into the cedar grove. Silently, he followed.

There was a Shinto shrine. The woman sat down on a flat rock beside two moss-covered statues of shrine dogs. "This is the coolest spot. Even in midsummer, there's a cool breeze."

"Are all the geisha here like that?"

"Somewhat. Some of the older ones are quite lovely." She cast her gaze down and spoke brusquely. He thought the dusky green of the cedars reflected on her neck.

Shimamura looked up at the top branches of the cedars. "It's all right. My strength has left my body—it's funny."

The cedars were so tall, they could only see the tops by bending backwards. The straight trunks stood side by side, the dark leaves blocking the sky. The stillness resounded. The tree Shimamura was leaning against was among the oldest. For some reason, the branches on the north side were all dead with the ends broken off. What remained of the branches looked like rows of stakes protruding from the trunk, with points outward like the fierce weapon of a god.

The woman was gazing at the distant river where the sunset was reflected. She felt awkward. "Oh, I forgot. Here's your tobacco," the woman said, trying to lighten the mood. "When I went back to your room a little while ago, you weren't there. I was just wondering where you were, when I caught sight of you climbing the mountain alone with such vigor. I could see you from the window. It was so funny. You seemed to have forgotten your tobacco, so I brought it for you."

She took out his tobacco from her kimono sleeve and lit a match.

"I wasn't very nice to that girl."

"That's the guest's choice—when to have her leave."

The water flowing in the rock-filled stream had a sweet, rounded sound to it. Through the cedar branches they could see the mountain crevices beyond beginning to darken.

"Unless she were as good as you were, afterwards when I met you I would feel awkward thinking you knew I'd been with her."

"Don't bring me into it. You're just a bad loser." The woman spoke as if with scorn, but a feeling different from before she had called the geisha passed between the two of them.

When Shimamura realized that from the beginning all he wanted was this woman and that he was making his usual roundabout approach, he felt, on the one hand, a great distaste for himself, while the woman appeared to him all too beautiful. After she had called him into the shadows of the cedar grove, something seemed to have deserted her cool figure.

Her narrow, pert nose looked lonely, but her small budlike lips beneath were smooth and they bulged and contracted like a beautiful circle of leeches. If they had been wrinkled or the color had been bad, they would have looked unclean, but they were wet and glistening. The corners of her eyes were purposely drawn straight out without rising. Her eyes were somehow strange, but her dense eyebrows, which tended to droop, surrounded them pleasantly. The contours of her face were ordinary, but her chin was like white porcelain with a faint reddish blush and there was little fleshiness at the base of her neck, so rather than call her a beauty, one would say she was pure.

For a woman who was accustomed to serving, she thrust out her chest in a rather forward manner.

"Look! The sand fleas have come out!" She stood up, brushing the skirts of her kimono.

That night about ten o'clock, the woman shouted Shimamura's name from the hallway, and tumbled into his room as if she had been thrown. Suddenly falling against the desk, she scattered the things on top with groping, drunken hands. She gulped some water.

The woman had gone out to meet some men she had become acquainted with at the ski slopes that winter. She was invited to their inn. They called in geisha and had a raucous time. She said they had gotten her drunk.

She rolled her head and rattled on. "I'm sorry. I shouldn't be here. I'll come back. They'll be looking for me, wondering where I am. I'll come again later." She staggered out the door.

An hour later he heard her confused footsteps as she seemed to bump and stumble along the hallway.

"Shimamura! Shimamura!" she screeched. "Oh, I can't see anything. Shimamura!"

It was obviously the voice of the naked heart of a woman calling her man. Shimamura was caught off guard. But it was a shrill voice that was surely echoing throughout the inn, so, flustered, he stood up. The woman stuck her fingers through the paper in the sliding partition and grabbed the frame. Then she collapsed against Shimamura. "Oh, here you are." She sat down in a tangle, leaning against him.

"I'm not drunk. How could I be? It just hurts. It hurts. I'm sober. Oh, I want some water. I shouldn't have drunk those rounds of whiskey with them. It gets to me. It hurts. They bought some cheap liquor. I didn't know it." She kept rubbing her face with her palms.

The sound of the rain outside suddenly grew fierce.

The woman faltered if he loosened his arm the least bit. He held her neck so close that her coiffure was crushed against his cheek. His hand was inside the neck of her kimono.

She did not respond to his request. The woman folded her arms to bar the way to what Shimamura sought, but, numb with drunkenness, she had no strength.

"What's this? Damn you. Damn you. It won't move—this arm!" She suddenly put her head down on her own arm.

Startled, he let go. There were deep tooth marks on her arm.

She gave herself up to his hands and began doodling. She said she was writing the names of men she liked. She wrote twenty or thirty names of movie and stage actors, then she wrote "Shimamura" over and over.

The pleasing bulge in Shimamura's hand gradually grew hot.

"Oh, it's all right. It's all right." He spoke serenely. He sensed something motherly in her.

The woman was suddenly in pain again. She writhed and stood up, but fell prostrate in the far corner of the room. "No, no. I'm going. I'm going."

"You can't walk. And it's pouring outside."

"I'll go barefoot. I'll crawl home."

"It's too dangerous. If you're going home, I'll take you."

The inn was on a hill. The slope was steep.

"Why don't you loosen your obi? You should lie down and sober up a bit."

"No, that won't work. I'm used to it this way." She sat up straight, and thrust out her chest, but her breathing was labored. She opened the window and tried to vomit, but nothing came out. She continued to stifle the urge to cringe and writhe. Then, every so often she would say she was leaving, as if to assert herself. It was soon past two o'clock in the morning.

The woman turned her face away, to hide from Shimamura, but finally thrust out her lips fiercely toward him. But after that, babbling, complaining of the pain, she repeated, time and again, "No, it won't work. It won't. Didn't you say 'Let's be friends'?"

Shimamura was struck by the sharp echo. The strength of her will as she furrowed her brow trying to control herself was enough to put him off. He even wondered if he should keep his promise to the woman.

"I don't regret anything. I'll never have any regrets. But I'm not that kind of woman. I'm not. Didn't you say yourself that it wouldn't last?"

She was half numb with drunkenness.

"I'm not at fault. *You* are. You gave in. You're the weak one. Not me." As she ran on, she bit her sleeve to stifle the joy.

In a moment she was quiet as if deflated. Then she jumped up as if recalling something. "You're laughing, aren't you? You're laughing at me."

"I'm not laughing."

"You're laughing deep in your heart. You may not be laughing now, but you'll surely laugh later." The woman lay facedown and sobbed.

But when she stopped crying, she began to talk in detail about herself, gently, in a friendly manner, but as if for herself. The pain of her drunkenness seemed to have disappeared, as if she had forgotten it. She did not bring up what had just happened.

"Oh, I've been so busy talking, I didn't realize." She smiled.

She said she had to leave before daylight. "It's still dark, but people around here get up early." She arose several times and opened the window. "I can't see anyone yet. It's raining this morning. No one will be going out to the fields."

Even after the roofs of the houses on the mountains and foothills across the way began to appear in the rain, the woman seemed unwilling to leave. However, she fixed her hair before the people at the inn got up and, afraid that people might observe Shimamura seeing her off at the entrance, she slipped out hastily, as if escaping.

When the woman lifted her head, he could see through her thick white makeup that her face had turned red from her eyelids to her nose, where Shimamura's palm had been pressed. While this made him think of the chill of the snow country nights, the deep black of her hair felt warm.

A dazzling smile appeared on her face, but she tried to suppress it. Even as she did so, Shimamura's words seemed to gradually permeate her body. Perhaps she was recalling the time they were together before. She sullenly hung her head, and Shimamura could see down the nape of her neck that even her back had turned red, as though a fresh, wet nakedness had been exposed. It may have been the harmony with the color of her hair that made him think so. Her hair in front was not fine and soft; it was combed back in bold strokes without a single stray hair. It had a luster like a heavy, black mineral.

The reason that Shimamura had been surprised earlier, saying it was the first time he had touched such cold hair, was not because of a chill; he wondered if it was the quality of the hair itself. As he gazed at her again, the woman began to count on her fingers as she sat at the *kotatsu*. It seemed she would never stop.

"What are you figuring?" he asked, but she continued to count silently.

"May twenty-third, right?"

"Oh, you're counting the days. Remember July and August are two long months in a row."

"It's the one-hundred-ninety-ninth day. It's been exactly one hundred ninety-nine days."

"It's the midnight train for Tokyo." She stood up at the sound of the steam whistle and flung open the paper partition and glass door with a rough, determined air. She sat in the window with her body leaning against the railing.

The cold air rushed into the room. As the echo of the train trailed off in the distance, it began to sound like the night wind.

"Hey! Aren't you cold? You fool." When Shimamura got up and walked toward her he found there was no wind.

The night scene was severe, as if the sound of the expanse of snow freezing were echoing deep within the earth. There was no moon. The unbelievably numerous stars appeared so vividly that they seemed to be falling, vain though their speed might be. As the clusters of stars approached, the sky deepened with the distant color of night. The ranges beyond ranges of the border mountains had grown indistinct and instead taken on the weight of a great mass. Everything was in harmony, clear and still.

When she noticed Shimamura approaching, the woman leaned out over the rail. It was not out of weakness. With this night as a setting it was the most stubborn pose she could have adopted. Not again, Shimamura thought.

Although the mountains were black, in an instant they appeared white with the bright snow. Then the mountains began to seem like sad, transparent entities. The sky and the mountains lost their harmony.

"Close the window."

"Let me stay like this a little longer."

The village was half-hidden in the shadow of the shrine grove of cedars, but the lights of the village, not ten minutes away by car, grew startlingly bright.

This was the first time Shimamura had ever felt such coldness before in the woman's face, the window glass, the sleeve of his own dressing robe—everything he touched.

Even the mats beneath his feet were growing cold, so he started to go to the bath alone.

"Please wait. I'll go too." This time she followed him meekly.

A male guest at the inn came in as the woman was placing in a box the clothing Shimamura had taken off and tossed down, but when he noticed that the woman had crouched before Shimamura's chest, hiding her face, he said, "Oh, excuse me."

"That's all right. We'll go to the other bath," Shimamura said promptly. Naked, he picked up the box and went to the women's bath next door. The woman naturally followed as if they were a married couple. Without speaking and without looking back, Shimamura jumped into the bath. Relieved, he felt a laugh bubble up in him, so he noisily rinsed his mouth at the spout.

After they returned to the room, the woman lifted her head as she lay down and pushed up her side locks with her little finger. "This is sad," was all she said.

When he drew close to peer at the woman, wondering if her dark eyes were half-open, he realized it was her eyelashes that made her look that way.

The nervous woman did not sleep a wink.

Shimamura awoke to the sound of a woman's obi being tightened.

Even after she finished tying the obi, she stood up, sat down, and walked around watching the window. It was the kind of restlessness, the irritable pacing, that occurs in nocturnal animals that fear the morning. A bewitching wildness was welling up within her.

He could see the woman's red cheeks. Had the room grown light? Startled, he was taken by the vivid red color.

"Your cheeks are all red. It's so cold."

"It's not because it's cold. I took my makeup off. As soon as I get in bed I get warm all the way to my toes," she said as she faced the mirror. "It's finally light outside. I'm going home."

Shimamura looked toward her, then shrank back. The depths of the mirror reflected the white snow. And the woman's red cheeks floated amid the snow. The pure, clean beauty was inexpressible.

Was the sun about to rise? The brilliance of the snow in the mirror increased as if it were burning cold. And with it the purple-black luster of the woman's hair in the mirror grew deeper.

JMH

ABOUT THE TRANSLATORS

LANE DUNLOP, advisory editor of *The Literary Review*, has been published widely in literary journals. He is the translator of *A Late Chrysanthemum: Twenty-one Stories from the Japanese* and *The Paper Door and Other Stories by Shiga Naoya*. His latest translation is *Floating Clouds*, a novel by Hayashi Fumike.

J. MARTIN HOLMAN, a graduate of Brigham Young University, did his graduate work in Japanese literature at the University of California, Berkeley. He has translated *The Old Capital* and *The Dancing Girl of Izu and Other Stories*, both by Kawabata. He teaches Japanese language, literature, and theater at the University of Missouri and directs the Bunraku Bay Puppet Troupe. He lives in Columbia, Missouri.